KU-634-764

On the spot, Cat knew she couldn't back down. It mattered too much. "I want love. I want marriage. I want a family," she said—and watched the color drain from his face.

She didn't need any more answer than that.

"I don't want to marry anyone. I don't want to get married." He shook his head. "Not on your life." The slow shake of his head and the clear honest look in his eyes told her as much as his words did.

She didn't need it spelled out any more clearly.

She felt a leaden weight in the pit of her stomach, but she managed very politely to say, "Thank you." Then she turned and walked away.

"You're not mad, are you?" Yiannis called after her.

She didn't turn. "Of course not." Mortified. Humiliated. Devastated. She kept walking.

"Good. Want to get a drink later?"

No, she did not.

Even now she could still remember the hot and cold of impotent fury and humiliation that had swept over her in successive waves even after she'd left her grandmother's and driven back to her own place. She'd named their children and he'd thought she was someone just to have a drink with!

So much for enchanted evenings. So much for true love and all the rest of her song lyric pipedreams.

So much for Yiannis Savas.

Award-winning author **Anne McAllister** was once given a blueprint for happiness that included a nice, literate husband, a ramshackle Victorian house, a horde of mischievous children, a bunch of big, friendly dogs, and a life spent writing stories about tall, dark and handsome heroes. 'Where do I sign up?' she asked, and promptly did. Lots of years later, she's happy to report the blueprint was a success. She's always happy to share the latest news with readers at her website, www.annemcallister.com, and welcomes their letters there, or at PO Box 3904, Bozeman, Montana 59772, USA (SASE appreciated).

Recent titles by the same author:

THE NIGHT THAT CHANGED EVERYTHING
HIRED BY HER HUSBAND
THE VIRGIN'S PROPOSITION

SAVAS'S WILDCAT

BY
ANNE McALLISTER

All the characters in this book have no existence outside the imagination of the author, and have no relation whatsoever to anyone bearing the same name or names. They are not even distantly inspired by any individual known or unknown to the author, and all the incidents are pure invention.

First published in Great Britain 2012
by Mills & Boon, an imprint of Harlequin (UK) Limited.
Harlequin (UK) Limited, Eton House, 18-24 Paradise Road,
Richmond, Surrey TW9 1SR

ISBN: 978 0 263 22678 2

Harlequin (UK) policy is to use papers that are natural, renewable and recyclable products and made from wood grown in sustainable forests. The logging and manufacturing process conform to the legal environmental regulations of the country of origin.

Printed and bound in Great Britain
by CPI Antony Rowe, Chippenham, Wiltshire

SAVAS'S WILDCAT

CHAPTER ONE

"YIANNIS?"

The voice came from far away—somewhere near his mouth, Yiannis decided, which was when he realized he had the receiver upside down against his ear. He rolled onto his back and fumbled to turn it right side up.

"Yiannis? Are you there?"

Ah, yes. Better. Louder, at least. He still didn't have his eyes open. They were gritty and he was stiff all over.

"Yeah. 'M here." His voice was like sandpaper, too, rough and sleep-fogged. No surprise since it felt like he'd barely fallen into bed.

"Oh, dear. I've wakened you. I was afraid of that."

He recognized the rueful voice now. It was Maggie, his ex-landlady and current tenant who lived in the apartment over the garage of the old beach house he'd bought from her almost three years ago. He knew she hated to ask him for anything. Maggie was as independent as they came. For her to call at this hour—whatever the hell hour it was—he knew it must be important. Maybe the roof had blown off?

"What's wrong? What happened?" He usually didn't have this much trouble with jetlag. But he'd spent more than thirty hours getting back from Malaysia and his head was pounding. He squeezed his eyes tight shut, then forced them open again.

It was light. Not bright, though, thank God. Through the half-open blinds he could see early morning fog. The California coast was thick with it until the heat of the day burned it off. Yiannis squinted at the clock. It wasn't yet seven.

"Nothing's happened. Well, not to the apartment," she answered. He heard hesitation in her voice. "I have a favor to ask." But she still sounded a little reluctant.

Yiannis shoved himself up against the headboard of his bed and said firmly, "Whatever you want."

When he'd made an offer on her Balboa Island house the realtor had said nervously, "The owner wants to remain as your tenant. In the apartment over the garage," she'd qualified quickly. "It's a condition of the sale." One she obviously hadn't looked happy about.

But, when he'd considered it, Yiannis decided it could be a good thing. After all, an eighty-five-year-old tenant was likely to be far less noisy and troublesome than most of those who would be drawn by Balboa's Southern California kick-back lifestyle.

"Give her a six month lease," the realtor had advised.

But Yiannis had actually offered to let her stay in the house while he moved into the adjoining apartment. He liked the property. Where he lived on it wasn't a pressing concern. Maggie had said no.

She was "downsizing," she had insisted. Climbing stairs would be "good exercise."

So as she'd wanted, he'd moved into the house and Maggie had taken the apartment over the garage. It had worked out well for both of them. Yiannis traveled for his business of importing and exporting fine woods for custom furniture makers. Maggie never went anywhere. She kept an eye on things while he was gone. He added to her postcard and tea towel collection from all over the world. She made him cookies and the occasional home-cooked meal when he was home.

She could stay forever as far as he was concerned. Maggie was not only a perfect tenant, having her there meant he didn't have a lot of extra space for house guests. The Savas family had long ago proved itself infinitely expandable. And while Yiannis appreciated his family's warmth and magnanimity, he didn't appreciate having relatives foisted on him every time he turned around.

He liked his family—but at a distance. A continent between them seemed about right.

Right before he'd headed to Southeast Asia two weeks ago, he'd been able to tell Anastasia, one of his triplet cousins, who had rung him wondering if he'd have "room for all of us" for spring break, that gee, no, he didn't. He smiled now at the memory.

Then he flexed his shoulders and swung his legs out of the bed, and stood up. "Whatever your heart desires, sweetheart," he said to Maggie. "Especially if it's tea towels," he told her. "I brought you half a dozen."

"Good heavens!" She laughed. "You spoil me."

"You're worth spoiling. What do you need?" He squinted out the back window. The roof still seemed firmly attached. But he was always happy to change a light bulb or repair a latch or carry her groceries up to her apartment, though at seven in the morning, he doubted that was the problem.

Maggie sighed. "I tripped over a stupid rug and my own feet this morning and I fell. I wonder if you'd give me a ride to the hospital."

"The hospital?" Yiannis felt as if he'd been punched. "Are you all right?"

"Of course," Maggie said briskly. "Just having a little trouble with my hip," she said. "I called. They said I should get it x-rayed."

"I'll be right there." Even as he spoke, he was pulling on his old Yale sweatshirt. Then he yanked on a pair of jeans and stuffed his bare feet into a pair of worn deck shoes. Less than a minute later, he was pounding up the steps to Maggie's apartment and letting himself in.

She was sitting on the sofa with a disgusted look on her face. Her white hair was pulled up into a neat bun at the back of her head. "Sorry about this. I don't like to trouble you."

"Not a problem. Can you walk?" He crouched down beside her.

"Well, I don't expect you to carry me!" She pushed herself up, wincing as she did so.

"I can carry you," Yiannis said. She weighed about as much as the decorative fishing net she had hung on one wall.

"Nonsense," she said, but when she tried to take a step, she gave a little gasp and would have fallen if he hadn't grabbed her.

"We should probably call an ambulance," Yiannis said grimly. But instead, he swung her up into his arms and carried her down the stairs to the garage where both his Porsche and her Ford sedan were parked side by side. He stopped.

Maggie sighed. "We'd better take my car," she said, a note of regret in her voice.

Yiannis grinned. "You don't want to show up at the hospital in the Porsche?"

"I'd love to," she said. "But you don't have room for a car seat."

He almost dropped her. "What?"

"We'll need the car seat. I've got Harry."

"Harry?" *Who the hell was Harry?*

"Misty's baby," she explained. "You remember? You've met him."

He remembered Misty. She was Maggie's late second husband Walter's granddaughter. No real relation to Maggie at all, but as far as Maggie was concerned, Misty was "family." Mostly, though, she was a flirt and a flake and, now that he recalled it, an unwed mother.

An airy-fairy surfer girl with long blonde hair, a deep tan and wide vacant blue eyes, Misty was beautiful but irresponsible. Age-wise, he figured she was about twenty—except emotionally, where she seemed more like seven. The world always revolved around Misty. Yiannis was appalled when he'd heard she had a child.

"Who's raising whom?" he'd asked Maggie.

She'd rolled her eyes at the time. "Maybe he'll be the making of her."

Yiannis hadn't thought it likely. But he did remember a scrap of a human wrapped in a blanket from one of Misty's visits a few months back.

"What do you mean, you've got Harry?" he said now.

"He's asleep in the bedroom. Don't worry. You can wake him. He won't fuss. Much," she added, and gave him a look that was, he was sure, meant to be reassuring. It merely looked hopeful.

"That's comforting," Yiannis said drily. He cast a look of longing at the Porsche as he edged past it and carried Maggie to the passenger side of her own car. "Where's Misty? Or shouldn't I ask?"

Now as he opened the door and tried to settle her in the passenger seat without hurting her, she said through gritted teeth, "She went to talk to Devin."

The baby's father. Yiannis remembered that name. He had never met Devin. Didn't think much of his taste in women certainly. But all he really knew was that Devin was in the army.

"There. I'm fine now," Maggie said, giving a little shudder. She looked white around the mouth, and Yiannis was worried.

"You're not going to faint," he told her. It wasn't a question. It was halfway between a command and a plea.

"I'm not going to faint," Maggie assured him. "Go back and get Harry. My car keys are in the rooster bowl on the kitchen bookshelf."

Yiannis took the stairs two at a time, snatched the keys out of the bowl and then went into the bedroom where Misty had apparently set up some sort of traveling crib affair for her sleeping baby. Yiannis supposed he should give her some credit for that—a car seat and a crib.

He'd have expected Misty to just dump the baby on Maggie for the day without any provisions at all. Maybe she was growing up.

The baby was stirring as Yiannis approached the crib. His dark head bobbed up and he looked around. Yiannis didn't know how old he was. Under a year, he thought. He remembered Misty being big as a whale and grumpy about it at the beginning of last summer. So Harry must have been born in the middle of it.

"Hey there, Harry old man." He made his voice cheerful as he peered over the top of the crib.

Harry pushed himself to a sitting position and looked up. When he didn't see whomever he'd been expecting, his little face crumpled.

Oh, God, tears.

"None of that," Yiannis told him firmly, snatching the boy up before he could even begin to emit a wail. Harry looked at him, startled, his blue eyes wide but, fortunately, tearless. "Let's go find your grandma," Yiannis said and wedging the baby on one hip, he locked the door and pounded down the stairs.

Harry didn't utter a sound—until he saw Maggie, whereupon he let out a warbling sound and held out his arms to go to her.

"Oh, honey, I can't take you." Maggie looked as distressed as Harry. "Did you change him that fast"

"What?" Yiannis had opened the back door of the car and was trying to figure out the logistics of getting Harry into the car seat.

"He just got up. He'll be wet."

Yiannis believed that. "We have to get you to the hospital."

"I can wait," Maggie assured him. She gave him a sweet hopeful smile.

Yiannis returned a glare. But he backed out of the car and studied her through the window to the passenger seat. She had her hands folded in her lap.

"You're enjoying this," he accused her.

Maggie gave a little sniff. "I'm not enjoying my hip hurting."

He grimaced guiltily because, of course, that was true. But still he scowled. "Making the most of a bad situation then."

She dimpled. "Something like that."

"You think I can't change a diaper?"

"I think you can do anything," Maggie said blithely, which was of course the right answer.

It was also true—and he'd prove it. "C'mon, Harry. Give us a minute," he said gruffly to Maggie and headed back toward the apartment.

It wasn't that he'd never changed a baby before. Hell, he'd changed a thousand of them. Well, maybe not that many, but when you came from a family the size of his—despite the fact that he was second youngest of his parents' children—you didn't escape babysitting. There were always cousins and nephews and nieces to be fobbed off on the unsuspecting—not to mention, unwilling—bystander.

Now he made short work of Harry's damp diaper and redressed the boy quickly. Apparently changing babies was like riding a bike. You didn't forget, even if you wanted to. And Harry was reasonably cooperative. He only flipped over and tried to escape twice, and Yiannis had always had quick reflexes.

"There you go," he said to the baby. "Now let's get your grandma to the hospital."

He scrawled a note and left it on the kitchen table for Misty telling her where they were and to feel free to come and get Harry. Then, carrying the baby, he went back down to the garage.

Harry bounced against Yiannis's hip and grinned and waved his arms and clapped his hands at his grandmother who returned the salute and the smile.

"You are a man among men," she told Yiannis as he put the boy in his car seat and figured out how to strap him in.

The nearest hospital was just up the coast a few miles. Yiannis had never been there before, but Maggie knew it well.

"It's where Walter died," she said.

"You're not going to die," Yiannis said, his jaw tight with conviction.

Maggie laughed. "Not today."

"Not any time soon." He wouldn't permit it. He didn't say anything else, just focused on getting to the hospital as quickly as he could. When they arrived, he pulled into the emergency area and went to get a wheelchair. But before he could, an orderly and a nurse appeared. They efficiently bundled Maggie into the chair and started into the building with her.

"You can fill out the paperwork as soon as you've parked," the nurse told him.

"I'm not—" he began, but they had already disappeared inside the building leaving him alone.

Well, not quite alone. He had Harry.

He was bouncing up and down in his car seat and making

cheerful noises. He even smiled when Yiannis bent down to look in at him.

Yiannis managed a semblance of a smile of his own. "Come on," he said, going around and getting back into the car. "Let's go find a parking place."

By the time he did, then extracted Harry from the car seat and went back to the emergency room, Maggie was nowhere to be found.

"They've taken her to x-ray," the lady at the admissions desk beamed at Harry. "Aren't you a cutie? How old is he?" she asked Yiannis.

"I don't know."

Her brows lifted in surprise.

"He's not mine."

"Ah, well. Too bad," she said. Yiannis didn't think so, but he didn't bother saying it. "They'll be back shortly. She did all the paperwork herself, so you're home free," the receptionist said. "You can wait here—" she pointed to a busy waiting room where someone was coughing and someone else looked decidedly bloody "—or in the room we put her in."

Harry was wiggling. Yiannis didn't think waiting in a room where Harry couldn't touch things was going to work. "We'll go for a walk." He gave her his mobile phone number. "Call me when she's back."

In the meantime, he would wander around outside with Harry and make a few calls of his own. He'd been out of the country, scouting out wood suppliers for the past two weeks. He'd dealt with emails while he was gone, but he had a dozen or more phone calls to return. So he played back his messages and began to return his calls, all the while letting Harry crawl around the grass, while he waited for Maggie to be ready to go home.

He was on his fifth call when the receptionist rang him. "Mrs Newell is back from x-ray."

He scooped Harry up and hurried back to the emergency room.

"Room three," the receptionist pointed them down the hall when they returned.

Room three was like all emergency rooms everywhere—filled with machines clinking and beeping as they surrounded the gurney on which Maggie lay. The nurse patted her on the arm. "I'll be right back," she said. "I just need to make the arrangements."

"Thank you," Maggie said to her. She almost didn't look like Maggie. The Maggie he knew was quick and energetic—and dressed. This Maggie was wearing a hospital gown. Yiannis's brows lifted.

Maggie grimaced. She looked strained and pale, though when she saw Yiannis, with Harry on his shoulders, she managed a smile.

"Hurting?" Yiannis guessed. But he grinned at her because she would expect that.

"A bit."

"They'll take care of it," he assured her. "You'll be fine in no time. Ready to run that marathon you're always talking about."

"That's what they tell me. Well, not the marathon part, but the rest." But she didn't sound happy about it.

Yiannis grinned, hoping she would, too. "Well, maybe a half-marathon, then," he said cheerfully. "It'll be okay," he assured her.

"They said that, too."

It wasn't like Maggie not to look at the bright side. He studied her closely. "Well, then—"

"It's broken."

He blinked. "What's broken?"

"My hip." Her voice was flat, resigned. "They're arranging surgery now."

"Surgery?" he echoed stupidly. Harry thumped him in the ear.

Maggie nodded. "For tomorrow morning."

Before the implications could begin to swim in his head, the nurse returned.

"It's all set," she said to Maggie. "They've got a room for you on the surgical ward. We'll be moving you there now. I've talked to Dr Singh's nurse. He'll do the replacement tomorrow morning at nine." As she spoke, she began to unhook Maggie from the monitors, eventually leaving in only the IV that was connected to the back of Maggie's hand. When she finished, she stuck her head out the door and called for one of the orderlies to come help.

Then she turned to Yiannis. "I'm sorry, but I'm afraid you can't come with her. Since the flu outbreak this past winter, hospital regulations don't permit children under fourteen on the ward."

"He's not mine."

"But you're holding him," the nurse pointed out.

"But—"

"If you have someone with you that you can give him to," she suggested, her voice trailing off, the implication obvious.

Yiannis shook his head.

The nurse shrugged and gave him a conciliatory smile. "Sorry. Rules, you know. Go home. Call her in half an hour. We'll have her settled by then. Or she can call you. Don't worry. We'll take good care of her."

"Yes, but—"

But the orderly came in then, and the nurse had other duties. She disappeared, leaving Yiannis holding the baby while he watched the orderly put Maggie's clothes in a bag, then stow it in the bottom of the gurney. In a minute he was going to wheel her down the hall and leave him here—alone—with Harry.

"Maggie?" he said, as the realization came home to roost.

"I know," Maggie said sorrowfully. "What will we do?"

"I don't think you're going to be doing anything," Yiannis said flatly.

Maggie looked guilty. "I should have realized."

"There's no way you could have known," Yiannis assured her. "Don't worry. It will be fine." He could cope for a couple of hours.

Maggie didn't look too sure.

"All set?" the orderly asked Maggie, hooking the portable IV unit to the gurney and beginning to wheel it toward the door.

"You can manage until tonight?" Maggie asked over her shoulder.

"Tonight?"

Misty wasn't getting back until evening? Yiannis tried not to sound annoyed, but he was. Not because of Maggie. But because it was just like Misty to impose like that. She was forever doing something and then expecting the whole world—mostly the world known as Maggie—to step in and pick up the slack. And now she'd taken off for the entire day and left her baby with an eighty-five-year-old. She'd probably never even considered that Maggie might fall and break her hip.

Well, he supposed, to be fair, if you knew Maggie, her falling and breaking her hip wouldn't be the first thing you'd think of. For an eighty-five-year-old she was well-nigh indestructible. But still—

He hurried after the gurney as the orderly pushed it down the hall. "Don't worry about it," he said firmly, catching up, Harry bouncing along on his shoulders, hanging on to fistfuls of his hair.

"I know it's an imposition."

"For you, darlin', I'll manage." He gave her a grin and a wink, determined that she shouldn't fret about him dealing with Harry. "Really. It'll be fine. But," he added, "you'd better give me her cell phone number just in case."

The least he would do was call and tell her about Maggie's surgery. And if he casually chewed darling Misty up one side and down the other for taking advantage of her step-grandmother's generosity, well, he figured it wouldn't hurt Misty a bit.

Of course he didn't say so. Maggie would not like him telling off Misty, not because of Misty's failings, but because she wouldn't want anyone to think she wasn't as capable as she'd ever been.

"She put her number in the rooster bowl on the kitchen shelf at home," Maggie said as they stopped at the elevator.

The orderly pressed the button. "This is as far as you go," he told Yiannis as the door opened. The orderly pushed Maggie inside.

"Don't worry," Yiannis said to Maggie. He reached out and gave her hand a quick squeeze. "We'll hold the fort, won't we, Harry?" He tugged on the little boy's foot. Harry giggled. "What time will she be back?"

"The fifteenth."

He hadn't heard her right. "Seven-fifteen?"

Maggie shook her head. "The fifteenth," she repeated.

Yiannis stared. *"What?"*

Maggie sighed. "Of March."

The elevator doors started to close.

Yiannis stuck his foot in between them. "That's *two weeks*!"

Maggie nodded. "She's hoping by the time she comes home, they'll have things worked out and when he gets back they'll get married. Actually I think she hopes they'll get married over there." Maggie managed to look bright at the possibility.

"Over where?"

"Germany."

This time when Harry hit him in the ear it was nothing compared to what he'd just heard. *"Germany?"*

"Please, sir. Keep your voice down," the orderly said sharply.

Yiannis did his best, demanding through his teeth, "Tell me Misty didn't go to Germany."

Maggie gave a helpless shrug. "I can't. She went. Well, she went to London first. But then Germany, yes. Devin has two week's R&R."

"And he didn't want to see his kid?"

"Er, I don't believe he knows about Harry."

"For God's sake!" Yiannis exploded.

"Sir!" The orderly looked censorious.

"I'm so sorry, dear," Maggie apologized.

Yiannis sucked in a breath. "It's all right," he lied because after all, it wasn't Maggie's fault. "I'll call her. Get her to come back."

"Not necessary," Maggie said. "I've taken care of it."

Thank God. He smiled his relief.

"You won't be alone," she added. Her smile brightened. "Cat is on her way."

Cat? Here?

Just when he thought things couldn't get any worse.

Yiannis opened his mouth to protest as the elevator doors began to slide shut.

"She'll be delighted to see you," Maggie promised as they closed to leave him staring at them.

Delighted to see him? Not hardly.

Catriona MacLean was the sexiest woman he'd ever met. She was Maggie's own granddaughter, as opposed to her step-granddaughter, the flaky Misty. Cat was the sensible granddaughter.

The one who hated his guts.

Taking a plane would have been quicker. The hour flight from San Francisco to Orange County, even with all that standing around airports beforehand, would have got her to her grandmother's bedside in far less time.

But Cat would need her car when she got to Balboa. Southern California wasn't meant for those who depended on public transportation. And Gran had said her surgery wasn't until tomorrow morning. So even though she hadn't been able to leave until after work, Cat knew she'd be there in plenty of time.

Besides, it wasn't a matter of life and death.

Yet.

The single renegade word snuck into her brain before she could stop it.

Don't think like that, Cat admonished herself, sucking in air and trying to remain calm as she focused on the freeway. Gran wasn't dying. She had fallen. She had broken her hip.

Lots of people got broken hips and recovered. They bounced back as good as new.

But most of them weren't eighty-five years old.

Which was another nasty thought that got in under her radar.

"Gran's a young eighty-five," Cat said out loud, as if doing so would make it truer. Exactly what a "*young eighty-five*" meant, she didn't know. But it sounded right.

And she knew she couldn't bear the thought of losing her grandmother.

Normally she never even thought about that sort of thing. Ordinarily Gran seemed just the same as she had always been—no different—or older—than when Cat had come to live with her twenty-one years ago. Margaret Newell had always been a strong, resilient healthy woman. She'd had to be to take on an angry, miserable orphaned seven-year-old.

She still was resiliant. Cat reminded herself. She just had a broken hip.

"She'll be fine," she said, speaking aloud again. "Absolutely fine."

But even though she said it firmly, she feared things might be changing. Time was not on her grandmother's side. And someday, like it or not, ready or not, time would run out.

But usually she didn't have to think about it. She didn't want to think about it, didn't want Gran's mortality thrust front and center in her life right now.

Or ever.

She was momentarily distracted by a pinging sound in the engine of her fifteen-year-old Chevy that she didn't think should be there. She didn't ordinarily depend on her car as her first choice of transportation. Foolish, perhaps, but in San Francisco, she didn't need to. The bus or Adam, her fiancé, took her wherever she needed to go.

Of course she had intended to get new tires before she came down to see Gran at Easter. But Easter was still a month away. So she hadn't got them yet. Besides, she was hoping Adam would come down with her. Then she might be able to put off getting them even longer.

But, in reality, Cat knew she should have got them last week. She should have been prepared. When your only living relative reached eighty-five years, you should always be prepared for anything. But "anything" seemed to imply "dying." And there she was back at the grimmest of possibilities again.

Damn it! She slapped her palms in frustration against the steering wheel.

"Don't die," she exhorted her grandmother now, though only Huxtable and Bascombe, her two cats fast asleep in the backseat, were there to hear her. They both slept right through her exhortation.

"You'll be fine," Cat went on as if her grandmother was listening. She infused her voice with all the enthusiasm she could muster. The cats ignored that, too. They ignored pretty much everything she did or said that didn't have to do with cans of cat food.

"It's no big deal, Gran," she went on firmly. But her voice wobbled and she knew she wouldn't convince anyone—especially no-nonsense Maggie Newell.

But she said them again. Practiced them all the way to Southern California because if she sounded convincing, then they would both eventually come to believe it. That was how it worked.

"You can make it happen," Gran had told her long years ago, "if you sound convincing."

And Cat knew for a fact it was true. She remembered those months after her parents had been killed and she had come to live with Gran and Walter. She'd been devastated, angry, a ball of seven-year-old misery. She'd hated everyone and she was sure she'd never be happy again.

Gran had sympathized, but had insisted that she try to look on the bright side.

"What bright side?" Cat had wanted to know.

"You have a grandmother and grandfather who love you more than anything in the world," Gran had told her with absolute conviction.

Cat hadn't been all that sure. It might be true, but it hadn't seemed like much compared to the love she'd lost at her parents' death. Still, she knew Gran had to be hurting, too. If Cat had lost her parents, Gran had lost her only daughter and her son-in-law. Plus she'd suddenly been saddled with an opinionated, argumentative child just when she and Walter were getting ready to retire and do what they wanted to do.

Still, Cat had wrapped her arms around her chest and huddled into a small tight cocoon of misery, resisting when Gran had slid her arms around her skinny shoulders and said, "Let's sing."

"Sing?" Cat had been appalled.

Gran had nodded, still smiling and wiping away the tear streaks on her own cheeks. "There's a great deal to be learned from musical comedies," she said firmly.

Cat hadn't known what a musical comedy was. She'd sat, resisting, stiff as a board. But Gran had persisted. She didn't have a good voice, but she had all the enthusiasm in the world.

She sang "Whistle a happy tune," and then she sang "Put on a Happy Face." She had smiled into Cat's unhappy one and kissed her nose. Then she'd sung "Belly Up to the Bar, Boys."

It was so absurd that even feeling miserable, Cat had giggled. And Gran had hugged her tighter, and then the dam inside her broke, and she remembered how she had by turns sobbed and laughed in her grandmother's arms. They'd sobbed and laughed together. And Cat could still feel the solid comforting warmth of her grandmother's arms around her that day. She longed to put her own arms around her grandmother now.

"It will be fine," she had told her grandmother on the phone that afternoon, refusing to let her voice crack. "We won't only sing. We'll dance," she vowed. "You'll be dancing in no time."

In her mind's eye she could see Gran dancing now. It made her smile—and blink away unshed tears. There. That was better.

Gran was right: you had to sound convincing to be believed—especially by yourself.

It did work. Cat knew it worked. At least in cases of misery—and in cases where the outcome was up to her.

If theme songs weren't one hundred percent foolproof it was because one time she'd been a fool and dared to believe in something she had no control over. Warbling "Whistle a Happy Tune" had got her through making new friends at her new school and in the Girl Scout troop. "Climb every Mountain" had helped her through swimming lessons and eighth grade speech. "Put on a Happy Face" had forced her to smile through teenage angst.

And if "Some Enchanted Evening" had failed her, it wasn't because there was something wrong with the song. There had been something wrong with the man.

She'd loved. But her love had not been returned. So she'd learned her lesson.

That was all behind her now. Now she had Adam who really did want to marry her, who smiled indulgently and shook his head and called her "Little Mary Sunshine," though sometimes she wasn't entirely sure he thought her sunshiny attitude was a good thing.

Adam was a banker, a very serious banker. Cat didn't mind serious. She didn't mind that he was a banker. It meant he was trustworthy. Dependable. The right sort of man to start a family with.

And more than anything Cat wanted a family.

She flexed her shoulders and tried to ease the kinks out of them. Bascombe mewed and poked his head between the two front seats. She wondered if he sensed that they were coming home. He'd been born on Balboa Island, had spent the first two years of his life there. They were south of Los Angeles at last, heading toward Newport and the beach. It was past one in the morning now and she was tired. Her only stop had been for gas in King City. Now she yawned so widely that she heard her jaw crack.

"Almost home," she told Baz. But the moment she said the words her stomach clenched, because once again the memories came flooding back, reminding her of the days she'd thought that Gran's old house would become her home again, that she'd marry and raise a family there.

And now—now it wasn't. She wasn't.

"Don't go there," Cat warned herself.

Because every time she did, she thought about Yiannis Savas and she grew hot and flustered and mortified all over again. Everything in her wanted to turn around and head straight back to San Francisco. For more than two years, she'd done exactly that—stayed well away from him.

But this time she couldn't because Gran was counting on her. She had to suck it up and act like the grown-up woman she was, and forget all about the airy-fairy fool who'd had her head in the clouds—or in the song lyrics—that had only brought her pain.

Determinedly she turned on the radio and tuned in the heaviest metal she could find. Baz hissed in protest.

"Sorry," she said, but he couldn't have heard her over the noise.

No matter. She needed it. Usually when she came down to visit Gran she tried to time it for when he was out of the city or, better yet, out of the country.

But this time she feared her luck wasn't that good.

When Gran had called she'd said Yiannis had brought her to the hospital. He was wonderful to her, of course. As always Gran couldn't say enough good things. Yiannis was "so thoughtful. So helpful. Taking care of everything until you get here."

What "everything" meant had not been specified.

"But I know you'll help him when you get here," Gran had said confidently.

The words had made the skin on the nape of Cat's neck prickle. Help Yiannis? Not likely.

Whatever needed doing, she would do it herself. She would

step in, take over, and that would be the last she would have to see of him. Fine with her. And she suspected it would be fine with him, too. Yiannis wouldn't want her around "getting ideas" the way she had the last time, would he?

Her cheeks started to burn again.

"I told him you'd help," Gran had said firmly when she hadn't replied.

Cat wasn't going to say what she was thinking. It wasn't the sort of thing you said to an eighty-five-year-old woman on her way to surgery the next morning. So Cat had made noncommital noises that could be construed as agreement.

"Couldn't be bothered to stay and see you settled in?" She did say that and it sounded about right. Yiannis wasn't one for commitment. Even the two hour variety.

"He just got back from Malaysia last night. He's exhausted. He needs his rest." Gran always managed to think the best of him.

But Cat had snorted. She knew Yiannis worked. But she also knew he played. Hard. Mostly what she saw Yiannis doing was playing—chatting up women. Charming them. Rubbing suntan lotion on their backs. Kissing them. Making them fall in love with him.

Then moving on to the next one.

Her fingers tightened on the steering wheel.

Poor Yiannis, she thought, annoyed. Yes, he might be exhausted. But she was willing to bet that if he was in his bed right now, he wasn't sleeping.

When she finally drove onto the island, the streets were deserted. Even the bars were closed. And while it ordinarily took ages to navigate Balboa's crowded main streets to get to Gran's, now she was pulling up to park in just a few minutes. All the lights were off at Yiannis's house on the front of the lot. But in the back, above the garage, there was a light on in

Gran's living room. Apparently Mr Savas had left the light on for her.

Grudgingly, Cat gave him one point for that.

She opened the car door and, in the unaccustomed silence, could hear the sounds of waves breaking against the shore. Getting out, she stretched, working the stiffness out of her cramped muscles and breathing in the damp sea air. Then, still rolling her shoulders, she opened the back door and reached in, scooping a cat up into each arm.

She carried them past Yiannis's house, through the small garden and up the stairs to the apartment. Then she opened Gran's door and shooed the cats in. Then she went back for her suitcase. Lugging it up the stairs, she tried to imagine when her grandmother would be able to climb them again.

Or *if* she would.

Something else she didn't want to think about.

Finally she reached the small porch, shoved open the door and heaved the suitcase inside. The cats loped toward her, then wove between her ankles, purring and meowing.

"Food," she translated and fished a can and their bowls out of her suitcase. While they were eating, she filled the litter box that Gran kept for their visits. By the time she finished Hux and Baz were back, looking for more food.

"Tomorrow," she told them sternly "Now just chill out and let's get some sleep."

They purred a bit more, but she resolutely ignored them. She was too exhausted to think. Her brain buzzed. Her eyes felt scratchy.

At least tonight, with Gran in the hospital, she wouldn't have to sleep on the sofa.

She went into the bathroom and stripped down to her T-shirt and underwear, too tired to dig through her suitcase for a nightgown. Then she brushed her teeth and shook her head at the sight of her bloodshot eyes in the bathroom mirror. Then, yawning, barely able to keep those eyes open, she pushed open the door to the bedroom, flicked on the light…

And stopped dead.

Yiannis—*and a baby*—were fast asleep on Gran's bed.

CHAPTER TWO

"You!"

At the squawk of feminine indignation and the sudden blinding overhead light, Yiannis threw up a hand to protect his eyes. Squinting, trying to figure out where the hell he was, he raised his head and saw two things—a sleeping baby on his chest and Catriona MacLean—in her underwear—gaping at him from the doorway.

He gaped right back, as dazed by the view as by the light. Fortunately he had the presence of mind to keep a hand firmly on Harry's back as the little boy began to stir. "Turn off the damn light," he commanded, though it rather pained him to do so. The view—as his pupils adjusted—was stunning.

"What?" Cat didn't move.

Harry whimpered.

"Turn off the flaming light, woman." Yiannis would have levered himself up and done it for her, but doing so would have disturbed the baby. "Unless," he added through his teeth, "you want him to start screaming. Again."

After three hours of virtually nonstop crying that had only tapered off what felt like minutes ago, Yiannis sure as hell didn't. All his nerve endings were frayed. Harry would probably still be yelling if Yiannis hadn't finally taken a page out of his brother Theo's book and settled the little blighter down on his chest.

That at last, had worked. But even as he finally quieted and drifted off, Harry still emitted intermittent heart-wrenching sighs that shuddered through his small frame. They made Yiannis feel guilty, though he wasn't the one who ought to be, heaven knew.

Fortunately the shuddering sobs were getting fewer and fewer. But he was not inclined to let anyone wake Harry again any time soon. He thought he might have to get up and shut it out for her when finally Cat did what she was told. The light flicked off. But he could still glimpse those memorable slender curves silhouetted in the doorway.

"What are you doing in Gran's bedroom?" Cat demanded.

What the hell did she think he was doing?

"Guess," he said irritably. "And shut the door while you're doing it. I'll be out when I'm sure he's settled."

"Huh." It was a snort that carried with it a truckload of doubt. But at least she finally pulled the door shut and remained on the other side of it.

Yiannis ground his teeth. He would have shut his eyes and gone back to sleep again, given half a chance, even though he'd doubtless have Cat's curves dancing on the insides of his eyelids. But he knew sleep was out of the question.

Cat would be back, even more annoyed than she was now—and she'd wake Harry. And while a part of him thought it would serve her right to deal with a screaming child, the sane sensible part knew that Harry didn't deserve to be awakened again.

Sighing, Yiannis worked a hand under Harry's belly and slowly rolled onto his side so he could slide Harry off onto the mattress. Harry made a soft whuffling noise. Yiannis froze.

The door cracked slightly. "Well?" a voice whispered.

Yiannis's teeth ground together. "Out!" And he held his breath, waiting until he was sure Harry was asleep again. Then he brushed a hand over Harry's downy head and started to slide off the bed when suddenly he felt something bounce onto it.

"What the—?"

A hard fur-covered head bumped against his shoulder. Yiannis reached out a hand and encountered a cat. A cat?

He grimaced. Oh, hell, yes. He remembered it now. Careful not to jostle the mattress, Yiannis eased himself off it, then snagged the cat up into his arms and, quietly as he could, he crossed the room and eased open the door.

Catriona MacLean was hastily zipping herself into a pair of baggy shorts. Pity. He would have liked to have seen more of those long bare legs. He remembered them well enough. Too well, damn it, for his peace of mind. The sight of them and the pert breasts that still peaked braless beneath her shirt were distractions that would only complicate things. More complications he didn't need.

When he dragged his gaze up to her face, he found her glaring at him. Deliberately and quietly he shut the door behind him, crossed the room and dropped the cat into her arms. "Yours?" he said acidly.

Her arms came around the cat and she buried her face against him for one long moment. Excellent. The feline covered her breasts.

"Mine," she said tersely. Then she lifted her flashing eyes. "What are you doing here? You and…and…your baby?" She almost stumbled over the last word.

Hell! She thought it was his?

"Not my baby," Yiannis said firmly.

An expression he couldn't quite interpret flickered across her features. "Then what are you doing with it?" she demanded.

"Him," Yiannis said. "His bed is here."

"His bed?" She blinked.

"Crib," Yiannis said. "Didn't you see it?"

"I didn't notice. I saw—you…and…" She gave a wave of her arm toward the bedroom.

"Harry."

She stared. Her mouth opened. And shut. "H-Harry?" There was a flicker of recognition colored by doubt.

Yiannis nodded. "Harry."

"Not…" She shook her head as her voice trailed off. Her gaze flicked to the closed door, then back to him. She hugged the cat tighter, as if he were some sort of shield she could hide behind. But of course he was a cat and had no intention of letting himself be used for anything at all. So he twisted and rippled right out of her arms and bounded away. Cats were like that. That's why Yiannis was a dog person.

"Misty's Harry?" Her tone was a mixture of doubt and disbelief.

"The very same."

He watched as Catriona MacLean digested that. The doubt and disbelief both wavered, then slowly vanished, followed by a look, not of shock, but of weary resignation. Her mouth tightened into a thin line. It looked as if she had the same opinion of Misty that he did.

Finally—something they could agree on.

"Where is Misty?" She looked around as if she might not have noticed Harry's mother in the room.

"Germany."

"What?" Then, "You're joking."

"Do I look like I'm joking?"

Their gazes locked, dueled.

Finally Cat accepted the truth and shook her head. "Oh, for heaven's sake." She sounded weary and disgusted, and her still pale face now showed an interesting blotch of freckles that stood out against her pallor. The indomitable Catriona MacLean looked worn out.

It was the first time he'd been given a glimpse of the Cat

beneath the fierce facade she presented to the world. Or at least to him. It reminded him of the day she'd told him her hopes—and he'd walked away from them.

He didn't want to think about that. Nor, apparently, did she. She must have realized that she was betraying her feelings, so she drew herself up sharply and wrapped her arms across her breasts.

"So what's he doing here?" she asked coolly. "With you?"

"He was staying with your grandmother."

"While Misty went to Germany?" Doubt dripped from her words.

"Apparently that's where Harry's father is."

Cat pursed her lips, the information obviously gave her pause for thought. Then she apparently had the same thought he'd had. "Why didn't she take Harry?"

"Maggie said Harry's dad doesn't know he is one."

Cat groaned. "So she's gone to tell him."

It wasn't a question. She sighed and shook her head. "Fat lot of good that will do." Then she reconsidered. "Well, I suppose it does her some good. Gets her away from her responsibility for a day or two."

"Week or two," Yiannis corrected. "Two, actually."

"What?"

"Quiet! You'll wake him up again. You don't want that. Trust me."

To his amazement, she immediately pressed her lips into a firm tight line and didn't say another word, just stared at him mutely. And he stared back, wondering why he did—why he always had. Catriona wasn't beautiful, God knew. And she wasn't his usual type. Ordinarily Yiannis went for blondes with long straight hair, small curvy girls who fit beneath his arm. Cat was nearly as tall as he was, more angles than curves, with vivid red curls, a million or so freckles, a tiny gap between her front teeth and green eyes that flashed fire rather than spoke of bedroom delights. Not his type at all.

And yet he'd wanted her from the moment he'd seen her.

Still did. And that was the annoying part.

He didn't want to be plagued by attractions that wouldn't go away. He'd steered clear of them his whole life. He'd had plenty of women tell him he was commitment-phobic. They all wanted to know what dire circumstance in his past had so damaged his psyche that he couldn't bring himself to get involved.

"He's not damaged. He's selfish," his sister Tallie had told one of them.

It was, essentially, the truth. Relationships required effort. They made demands. Took time. He wasn't interested. He liked his freedom, wanted to be unencumbered, forever footloose and free.

It was why Cat snarled and spat at him. They'd had three months together. Damn good months, he remembered. He'd never clicked with any woman the way he had with Cat, in bed and out.

But ultimately she'd wanted more than he'd been willing to give. And now, according to Maggie, she'd found someone who was willing. He found himself looking at her hand to see if she wore a ring.

She did. It flashed in the light as she moved. His jaw tightened.

"Impressive," he grunted.

She blinked. "What?"

"Never mind." More power to her, he thought grimly. She'd got what she wanted. And he didn't have to keep standing here. He was free to go. Smiling, he flexed his shoulders.

"Right," he said. "I'll be off then."

"Off? No!" The sudden urgency in her tone surprised him, as did the volume. So much for silence. Instantly Cat clapped her hand over her mouth, then warily uncovered it again after a long moment's wait didn't produce a wail from the bedroom. Then she said in little more than a whisper, "I mean, no. You can't."

"Can't?"

Cat shrugged awkwardly. "Well, I mean…he doesn't know me. He knows you!"

"He didn't know me fifteen hours ago."

"But he knows you now," she insisted.

"So?"

The color was high in her cheeks. "So you don't want him having a fit when he wakes up and finds a stranger here." She waved her hands. The ring flashed again.

Yiannis narrowed his eyes. "You mean *you* don't."

But she didn't admit that. She gave him a guileless look, then pursed her lips and raised her chin. "Children need continuity." She sounded like a public service pronouncement.

"Says who?"

"I deal with children every day. I'm a librarian."

"Then tell him to shush."

Her green eyes flashed. "Not a stereotypical librarian. I give programs. I tell stories with puppets."

"I'm sure Harry will love puppets."

She hugged her arms across her chest. "You're laughing at me."

"I'm not," he swore, but he did like watching her eyes flash. He always had.

"You are," she disagreed and gave him one of her disapproving looks. "But when he wakes up and doesn't know who I am, that won't be good for him."

"I'm not sure life has been particularly good for Harry."

Cat's mouth opened. And closed again. From her expression he thought she was considering what Harry's life was like.

Finally she sighed. "Poor Harry. Gran shouldn't have said she'd take him."

He frowned. "And that would have been better because?"

She flung her hands in the air. "Because then maybe for once Misty would act responsibly."

"I wouldn't count on it."

"No. Probably not. But I don't know what to do. I can't take him for two weeks! And Gran won't be able to."

"Misty's number is in the rooster bowl," Yiannis told her. "Maybe you'll have better luck getting hold of her than I did."

"I doubt it. Germany?" She shook her head. "I can't think why Gran would have agreed. She didn't even mention it when she called me."

"She didn't mention him to me, either—until I was putting her in the car."

At Cat's look of surprise, Yiannis shrugged. "Well, what was she going to do? Call social services and tell them to come and get this spare baby she couldn't take care of any longer?"

"Of course not, but—" Cat paused, considering. "I guess she didn't want to give you a chance to back out."

"Or you, either, obviously," Yiannis said.

"So, what are we going to do?"

Yiannis blinked. "We?"

"Oh, I forgot. You don't do responsibility, do you?"

"I'm here," he pointed out, irritated at how the veiled accusation stung.

"And leaving," she reminded him.

"You want me to spend the night with you?" He waggled his eyebrows suggestively.

"I do not. I know better than that," Cat snapped. "I'm only trying to think of what's best for Harry."

"Well, I did my bit. Maggie said you'd be taking over."

"It's not what she said to me! She said I should help you."

"You're her granddaughter."

"You're her landlord!"

"You're Harry's aunt. Or cousin. Or something."

"Not…technically. Misty is Walter's granddaughter. Not related to me."

"Or me," Yiannis pointed out.

There was a silence during which he could actually hear a wave break against the sand half a block away, could almost see thoughts forming in Cat's mind, though he didn't know what they were.

Finally she sighed. "Fine," she said abruptly. "Go. Take your freedom and leave. It's only what I'd expect." She started toward the bedroom.

Instinctively Yiannis blocked her way. "If you need me to stay, I'll stay."

Where the hell had that come from?

Cat stopped inches from him. Close enough that he could count her blasted freckles. Dark brows hiked haughtily on her forehead. "I don't *need* you at all!"

"But you're afraid Harry might," he persisted.

She shoved a hand through her hair. The diamond winked. "He might," she said grudgingly. "If he was that upset before, how upset will he be if he wakes up and finds yet another stranger here. But never mind. You're right. Harry is my responsibility. Of the two of us, I'm the one who should be taking care of him. Now—" she looked past him toward the front door, as if wishing him through it "—it's late. I've driven all the way from San Francisco. I'd like to go to bed. I'm tired."

Yiannis would like to go to bed, too. With her, damn it. He was a healthy red-blooded male, for God's sake. But thinking about it wasn't going to make it happen. So he shoved the thought away.

"You'd better hope Harry sleeps then," he told her.

"I hope Harry sleeps." She said it with enough fervency to make it sound like a prayer. "Good night." She brushed past him to put a hand on the bedroom door. "Turn out the light when you leave."

He'd been dismissed, but Yiannis didn't move. "Do you know anything about babies?" he asked.

Cat glanced back at him over her shoulder and gave a half-shrug. "I expect I'll learn."

"At Harry's expense."

"We'll be fine," she said stoutly. "I babysat once or twice when I was a teenager, and I deal with preschoolers all the time."

"Harry's not a preschooler."

"And I'm not a teenager. We'll cope."

He doubted it. He'd just been through a three hour Harry War Zone. At least he knew what to do. And he'd done a damn sight more babysitting in his life than she apparently had. Harry wasn't any docile cherub. He wriggled when you changed him, and he could crawl faster than lightning. She'd probably let him fall off the bed.

"Fine," he snarled. "I'll stay."

"What? No!"

"Oh, for God's sake. Two minutes ago you didn't want me to leave!"

"I over-reacted."

"Maybe," he said grimly. "But you haven't seen Harry at full throttle."

"Don't do me any favors."

"I'm not doing you any favors. I'm doing Harry a favor."

Cat opened her mouth as if she were going to dispute that. But apparently she thought better of it. She gave a casual lift of her shoulders and said, "If you think so."

In fact Yiannis thought he needed his head examined. He wanted to bed her, not spend the night with an eight-month-old. But he couldn't leave Harry to her mercies, could he? And she wasn't going to sleep with him anyway. Not the way she kept flashing that ring around. No, he was doing this for Harry—because she'd basically said she had no idea what she was doing. "I think so," he said shortly.

"Suit yourself," she said as if it were a matter of supreme indifference. "I'll make up the sofa for myself then."

And she brushed back past him to go and open the chest beneath the window next to the sofa.

He should have turned on his heel and gone straight into the bedroom. Of course he didn't. He did what he always did when she was around—watched her. And if he'd thought she was tempting before, the sight of Cat MacLean's lush bottom and long legs as she bent to pull out a sheet and summer weight blanket made Yiannis's body go on full alert.

Don't look, his sane sensible self told his rampaging libido.

But it was like telling himself to turn away from two speeding trains headed straight at each other, just about to crash. Only when she straightened again and tossed the sheet onto the sofa did he manage to drag his gaze away.

"What?" Cat demanded when he still stood there, his brain turning to mush while other parts of him felt more like hot steel.

He turned away abruptly, clearing his throat. "Nothing."

"Well, then?"

As if on cue there was a whimper from beyond the door.

Cat's eyes widened. "He wants you."

"He probably wants his mother."

"Then more fool he," Cat said. Yiannis totally agreed with her. "What's wrong with him? Is he hungry?" she asked, looking a bit nervous.

"Maybe. I gave him a bottle about eight." Fortunately he'd found plenty of formula when he'd gone through the cabinets. Either Misty or Maggie had thought ahead, thank God. But even so, he'd called his sister, Tallie, who had four kids of her own to ask what he was supposed to feed Harry and how often.

Predictably Tallie had laughed. "*You* have a baby?"

"I'm taking care of it. For the moment," he'd said.

"Moment. Yeah," Tallie had said doubtfully. But then she'd asked him dozens of questions, most of which he didn't know the answer to, about how old Harry was and what he was accustomed to eating. Given the little he had been able to tell her, he thought she'd given him reasonably good advice.

Harry hadn't cried those three hours because he was hungry. He had screamed because life was doing bad things to him—going where he didn't want to go, taking over, spinning seriously out of control.

There came now a long serious wail from the bedroom.

Yiannis knew exactly how he felt.

Crying wasn't an option.

But Cat rather wished it were.

Dear Lord, what a mess! Bad enough that Gran had broken her hip, that she was having surgery and would not be able to come back to her apartment for heaven knew how long. It wasn't even clear if she would be able to be on her own any longer at all.

It was, Cat would have thought, a worst case scenario.

But apparently not worst enough. Now she didn't only have her grandmother to worry about, Cat had Misty's perennial irresponsibility to factor in. And not just the sort of ethereal blend of flakiness and selfishness that Misty generally wafted about in. No, this was Misty's very solid, flesh and blood, one hundred percent real baby in the next room.

And Yiannis Savas, for good measure.

Looking every bit as handsome and appealing as he ever

had. He was still—damn him—able to make her pulses hammer, her body tremble and her common sense turn to mush.

A very large part of Cat wanted to bundle her cats back in her car and head straight back to San Francisco this very moment.

Of course she couldn't. She was Gran's only living relative. Gran was her responsibility, a responsibility she was perfectly willing to accept. She loved her grandmother. And she owed her as well.

Gran had been a shelter of comfort and strength at the worst time of Cat's young life. She knew she could never repay that. But she would do her best. So there was no leaving.

But there was no sleeping, either.

She should have fallen asleep the second her head hit the pillow. Instead she lay there, aware of the man in the next room, and tossed and turned for hours.

Sleep, Cat told herself firmly, trying to find a comfortable spot on Gran's seriously lumpy sofa. But she didn't. She thought about Yiannis.

And because that was as unlikely to be productive as ever, she forced her mind to other problems—her grandmother's future, which was too uncertain to have any useful thoughts about, and ultimately, Harry.

Harry she would be required to do something about. Soon.

Trust Misty to dump a baby on her.

Not that she didn't like babies—or at least, the *thought* of babies. But she had so little experience with them, whereas Yiannis—damn it, there he was again!—seemed to be able to deal with them. Or at least, if she credited his insistence that Harry had cried for three hours earlier in the evening, to persevere.

She would have to learn to persevere. She could. She'd been persevering with Misty ever since she'd come to live with Gran. Not the easiest of relationships, especially since Cat's permanent arrival on Gran and Walter's doorstep had meant Misty had had to share the limelight. Or should have.

Mostly it had meant that Misty did what she wanted and left Cat, five years older and decades more responsible, to mop up after.

Not, Cat reminded herself, determined to be fair—which Misty certainly never was—that Harry's mother had intended for her to take care of him this time.

In fact, Misty would probably have spun in her grave, if she'd been in one, at the thought of Cat *in loco parentis* to her son. She knew that more than anything Cat wanted a family, and Misty had never been one to share.

Certainly she wouldn't have knowingly shared Harry with Cat. She'd never even brought him around when Cat had come to visit Gran. Until tonight Cat had never met Harry.

And she'd barely caught a glimpse of him this time. If she recalled anything about him, she'd been struck by his thick dark hair—a trait he shared with the man whose bare chest he had been sleeping on.

The memory still had the ability to make her breath catch.

She had not expected Yiannis. Not here. Not tonight.

And certainly not on a bed, asleep with a baby in his arms.

She squeezed her eyes shut now, trying to blot out the memory. But she feared the sight would be emblazoned on the insides of her eyelids until her dying day.

It had once been the stuff of dreams.

Hopes and dreams crowded back—resurrected by the sight of him holding Harry—and pain she had resolutely put behind her, now stabbed her again. She tried to put them out of her mind, but whether it was the circumstances—he was here right now on the other side of a six inch wall with a baby in his arms—or her exhaustion, she couldn't seem to shut them out.

Couldn't shut him out.

"Stop it!" she muttered aloud and squeezed her eyes shut tight. But he really did seem to be on the inside of her eyelids.

She snapped them open and found herself nose to nose with Bas.

"Uh!" She picked him up and dropped him gently onto the floor. Then she sat up and scrubbed at her eyes. It didn't help. Nothing helped.

It had been like this since the day she'd met him.

She could remember it as though it had been yesterday, the afternoon she'd seen this lean, muscular guy with the wind-ruffled black hair and stubbled jaw sauntering down the street toward her. She'd been coming back from the grocery store, her arms full of bags, eager to get to Gran's and set them down. But at the sight of the most gorgeous man she'd ever laid eyes on, the weight of the grocery bags had meant nothing and she'd slowed her pace, wanting to look her fill before they passed on the street.

But he'd slowed, too—as if he were as taken with her as she had been with him. If an entire orchestra had risen up out of the pavement and begun playing "Some Enchanted Evening" she would not have been surprised.

Of course it had not been evening. But she'd granted fate poetic license. No one had ever accused Cat of lacking imagination. Before he reached her, she had imagined him pausing to smile and flirt a bit. They would talk, and, finding her a kindred spirit, he would ask her out. They would fall in love, get married, have three children and a golden retriever and live happily ever after right here on Balboa Island.

The trouble was, it had actually happened—the first bits. He had smiled. He'd flirted. He'd introduced himself. He had been coming to see her grandmother, interested in buying Gran's house. He'd asked her out. Once, twice. Half a dozen times. They'd clicked. It was exactly the way it was supposed to be.

He'd bought Gran's house.

It was perfect. Even the sex was perfect. Hot and intense and absolutely amazing. Of course it was, because they were perfect for each other. Cat knew she'd met the man she was going to spend the rest of her life with.

And then…

And then it fell apart.

It turned out that life was not a series of musical comedy song moments. Life was discovering Yiannis seeming a little distant whenever she talked about how she was longing to have a family of her own. Life was him changing the subject if the M word ever remotely cropped up in conversation. Life was him leaving for Singapore or Finland or Dar es Salaam. It was her waiting eagerly for him to come back from wherever and then getting an email saying he'd decided to spend a week on the beach at Goa and then go right on to New Zealand instead.

And then, of course, there had been Misty.

Misty had never met a man with cheekbones, a great smile and all the standard male equipment that she didn't like—and want.

And that went double if it was a man paying attention to Cat.

There wasn't a toy or a game or a boy or a man that Cat had first that Misty didn't consider fair game. Cat understood that.

She just hadn't thought Yiannis would take a second glance.

But if there had been any mistaking Misty jumping into his arms on the beach or sitting across an intimate table from him at Swaney's bar or coming out of his place at seven in the morning, there had been no mistaking his answer when

Cat had asked him point blank about where Misty stood—and she stood—in his life.

"Where do you stand?" He stared as if he'd never given it a thought.

She'd got a pretty good idea of the answer from his baffled echo of her question. But though her fingernails bit into her palms, she had nodded and hoped he might yet give her the answer she was hoping for.

Instead he'd countered with a question of his own. "Where do you want to stand?"

On the spot, Cat knew she couldn't back down. It mattered too much. "I want love. I want marriage. I want a family," she said—and watched the color drain from his face.

She didn't need any more answer than that. As far as she was concerned, Misty could have him. She'd said so.

"I didn't sleep with Misty," he told her. "She came by to pick up her sunglasses. She left them here yesterday and she wanted them before she went to work."

Cat had absorbed that, had allowed a flicker of hope to remain in her heart—until he said, "And I sure don't want to marry Misty." He grimaced at the thought. "I don't want to marry anyone. I don't want to get married." He'd shaken his head. "Not on your life." The slow shake of his head and the clear honest look in his eyes told her as much as his words did.

She didn't need it spelled out any more clearly than that.

She felt a leaden weight in the pit of her stomach, but she'd managed very politely to say, "Thank you." Then she turned and walked away.

"You're not mad, are you?" Yiannis had called after her.

She didn't turn. "Of course not." Mortified. Humiliated. Devastated. She kept walking.

"Good. Want to get a pizza later?"

No, she had not.

Even now she could still remember the hot and cold of impotent fury and humiliation that had swept over her in successive waves even after she'd left her grandmother's and driven back to her own place. She'd named their children and he thought she was someone to share a pizza with!

So much for enchanted evenings. So much for true love and all the rest of her song lyric pipe dreams.

So much for Yiannis Savas.

Less than three months later Cat took a job at a library in San Francisco.

Gran hadn't been pleased, but Cat had been adamant. Putting four hundred miles between herself and the man who had no interest in being her one true love seemed only sensible. Not that she'd said anything about that to Gran.

Her stupidity was her secret, and hers alone.

And she'd been careful to avoid him ever since because he unfortunately hadn't grown any less gorgeous or any more resistible. And even though she was an engaged woman now—with a man who wanted exactly the same things she did—as soon as she saw Yiannis the stupid song lyric feelings were still there.

That one single glimpse of him tonight, asleep on Gran's bed with Harry on his chest was like a kick in the gut. Those perverse misbegotten childish fantasies were not dead yet.

Furiously Cat flung herself over again with such force that she slipped right off the narrow sofa and landed on the floor.

"Oh, hell!" Wincing at the thud, she scrambled up onto the sofa and lay perfectly still, holding her breath, terrified that Harry would start crying or—worse—that Yiannis would appear in the doorway to demand what the devil she was doing.

A minute passed, then two. She didn't move. On the other side of the wall she heard a whimper, but no footsteps. She breathed again. Shallowly. Rolled carefully onto her side.

The whimpers were coming more emphatically now. Harry seemed to be working up a head of steam now, starting to cry.

The door to the bedroom opened. Yiannis stepped quickly out and shut the door behind him. The crying in the bedroom continued unabated.

Was he going to run off and leave her with a crying baby?

He didn't turn on a light, but padded silently across the living room, not even glancing her way. Holding her breath, Cat waited, fully expecting him to open the front door and let himself out.

Instead Yiannis opened the refrigerator. In its light she could see his sharp profile, the shaggy hair that fell across his forehead, his firm torso and muscular legs bisected only by a pair of light-colored boxer shorts. He snagged a baby bottle. Then the door closed again and he turned on the kitchen tap.

Cat eased her head up just enough to see past the arm of the sofa. She knew she should shut her eyes. But she was engaged now. She had a future and it didn't include Yiannis. So where was the harm?

Besides, the vision of Yiannis warming a baby bottle was too compelling to look away from.

"Want to feed him?" he asked suddenly.

Cat jerked. Then, mortified that he'd known she was watching, she tried to pretend his question had awakened her. "Wha—?" She raised up on one elbow to peer sleepily in his direction. "You woke me," she added for good measure.

"I'm sure." Clearly he didn't believe her protestation. And with Harry cranking up the volume in the bedroom, she couldn't pretend he was wrong. He shut off the tap and shook a bit of the liquid from the bottle onto his wrist.

"Old pro?" Cat couldn't help asking.

"I've fed a few." He carried the bottle back into the living room and held it out, but when she didn't make a move to reach for it, he only shrugged. "Get your beauty sleep," he said gruffly, and walked right past her. The bedroom door opened. Harry was endeavoring to wake the dead now. Then it closed again, softening the roar.

Moments later the crying stopped. There were occasional tiny hiccups, a slurp and a soft sigh. She heard Yiannis's voice murmuring as well.

It was that quiet yet deep voice she remembered from sharing a bed with him. Whispers. Suggestions. Sweet nothings.

Cat felt all her nerve endings awaken in response. She lay still and listened—to the murmurs, to the silence, to the sound of waves against the shore. Her whole body thrummed with awareness, even as Harry grew quiet for a time and in her mind's eye she could imagine him snug in Yiannis's arms.

She willed the image away. Shut her eyes. Thought of Gran, of what would happen after her surgery. Mustered up thoughts of Adam. Tried to imagine Adam holding a baby—*their* baby—close, cradling it in his arms.

But a hypothetical baby couldn't compete with the real one making sounds on the other side of the wall. She heard little whimpers and coos from Harry. Then a soft deep masculine voice replied. As if they were having a conversation.

Yiannis and a baby.

Cat's throat tightened. She swallowed, cleared it determinedly, thrust away the fantasies. They weren't real even if Harry was.

But then she heard another sound. No. Impossible. Her mind instantly rejected it. And yet—she strained to listen closer. Yes, she could still hear it. Soft. Rhythmic. Melodic.

Yiannis Savas was crooning a *lullaby* in the other room.

CHAPTER THREE

BY THE time the door opened to the bedroom again scant hours later, Cat had dragged herself up, got dressed and, most importantly, had her game face on.

She'd lain awake after the lullaby, trying not to contemplate the visions it evoked, reminding herself that Yiannis was still the same man and she was the same woman. Nearly three years might have passed, but they still wanted different things.

Just because he could give a bottle and lull a baby to sleep didn't mean he wanted one or two or three of his own.

Adam did. He'd said so.

She needed to remember that.

She had showered and dressed, then put on her going-to-the-hospital clothes—buff-colored canvas cropped pants and a peasanty sort of top in rusts and oranges and golds that was more eye-catchingly bright than her hair. It was a form of camouflage. Yiannis had delighted in running his fingers through it. Now she had it tamed, pulled back into a band so tight it made her scalp hurt. The pinch of it would be an extra reminder, she thought as she sat at the kitchen table, cradling a mug of coffee in her hands.

Now as the door opened, she turned a bright, if not entirely sincere, smile on the man who emerged—dressed, too, thank God—and the baby he held in his arms. Yiannis's jaw was gorgeously stubbled and she remembered that heavy-lidded gaze from the mornings she'd awakened next to him. Determinedly she steeled her emotions against the memory. "Good morning," she said briskly.

"Morning." His voice was still gravelly with sleep, but in it she heard a slight roughness she recalled from hearing through the wall as he had sung a lullaby scant hours ago.

"Did you sleep well?" She kept her tone bright. Maybe too bright. But if so, too late. The words were already out of her mouth.

He gave her a baleful look. "Oh, definitely." The look he gave her belied the words.

It wasn't her fault, she wanted to remind him. She wasn't the one who'd kept him up. That was Harry—and Harry wasn't hers. But she didn't want to go there with him this morning. Or any morning, for that matter.

So she just said cheerfully, "Good morning, Harry," turning her focus on the little boy. "Did you sleep well?"

Harry obviously knew she was talking to him. He turned and hid his face in Yiannis's chest.

Great. Another male who wanted nothing to do with her.

She would have reached out and tickled his bare toes, but that would mean coming into close proximity to Yiannis's midriff. And even though it was completely covered by a faded navy blue T-shirt this morning, she didn't want to get too close.

"I made coffee," she said, "If you want some."

Yiannis loved his morning coffee, and knowing that, she'd very nearly decided not to make a pot. But to prove she was an adult and it didn't matter, she had.

Now, though, the smile he gave her did such disastrous things to the beat of her heart that she was wishing she'd given it a miss.

"You are a godsend." He shifted the boy to his other arm,

so he could use his right hand to pour the coffee into a mug. "Thank you." The words were heartfelt and he raised the mug toward his lips.

Instantly Harry reached for it. But with complete ease, Yiannis shifted his body to keep Harry firmly ensconced and the hot coffee well out of the boy's reach.

Cat's brows lifted. "You're very good at that."

Yiannis blinked. "Good at pouring coffee?"

"At keeping the coffee away from him."

"Plenty of practice."

"All those little children you've got?"

"All those little nieces and nephews and cousins." He grimaced.

But she felt a prick of envy. "Really?" It occurred to her that while she'd been busy embroidering her fantasies of Yiannis as the father of her children, they'd never really talked about his family much.

"Hordes of 'em."

"Lucky you."

He grunted. "As long as they're somebody else's."

No, he definitely hadn't changed. But whether he liked kids or not, his ease with Harry was obvious. He moved easily around the kitchen, getting one of Harry's clean bottles off the counter and filling it with water, then deftly flicking the plastic lid off a tin of dried formula powder. It was only when he tried to measure scoops of the powder into the narrow mouth of the bottle while Harry squirmed in his arms that he had a bit of a problem.

Cat was glad to know there were limits to his expertise.

"Let me do that," she said, getting up and taking the measuring scoop from him. Their fingers brushed. Perversely—annoyingly—Cat's tingled at the merest touch. Good grief, it was like something out of a romance novel.

Minus the hero, of course. She fumbled the scoop and it

slipped through her fingers and fell on the counter. He handed it back to her.

Feeling like a fool, she stuck it in the tin again. "How many more?"

"Three." He watched as she dumped each in the bottle, standing so close that she could almost feel the heat emanating from his skin.

"Go sit down," she snapped, as she finished and put the nipple on the bottle. She shook the bottle energetically, still with her back turned, so she jumped when a hand snaked around and opened the drawer she was blocking.

"What are you—?"

"Just getting a spoon," he said in patient, soothing, highly irritating tones. "I need to feed him."

"The bottle—"

"That, too." His arm brushed against her as he extracted a spoon from the drawer. This time Cat managed not to jerk away, but she hated the awareness that wouldn't let her alone, and she was glad when he crossed the room to grab a jar of peaches from the counter top and then, finally, sat down at the table dangling Harry on his knee.

"I think there's a high chair sort of thing in the closet," Cat offered. "It clamps to the table. I've seen it before. Misty apparently left it here so she wouldn't have to lug a high chair back and forth. I gather she brings Harry to Gran's often."

Now she crossed the room and opened the broom closet. "Here it is." She pulled a metal and canvas contraption out. She was sure it wasn't rocket science to figure out how it worked, but it wasn't intuitively obvious, either.

But even as she stared at it, Yiannis said, "Give it here." He took it from her and at the same time thrust Harry into her arms.

"Wha—!" The squirming bundle that was Harry was heavier than she thought. Also he had a mind of his own. She almost dropped him before she got a firm grip and wedged him against her middle, then wrapped her arms firmly around him.

As she'd told Yiannis last night, she was used to preschoolers, not babies. It felt odd, holding this one. But it also felt every bit as right as she'd dared to hope it would feel, and she couldn't resist dipping her head to brush her nose and lips against Harry's downy head and breathe in the scent of baby shampoo and clean laundry.

Yiannis made quick work of opening, fitting and clamping the collapsible chair to the table top. Cat tried not to be impressed. Harry wriggled in her arms and turned to see who was holding him, then reached up and pulled at strands of her ruthlessly scraped back hair.

"Ouch!"

Yiannis looked up and grinned at Harry's fingers in her hair. "A man after my own heart."

Face burning at the memory of how she'd loved Yiannis's fingers in her hair, Cat tried to loosen Harry's.

"Let me."

Before she could protest strong masculine fingers were gently easing Harry's death grip. Yiannis's thumb and knuckles grazed her cheek, then she was free, and he was brushing her hair lightly off her face. She tried to remain immobile and indifferent.

She got fifty percent on that.

Yiannis's eyes met hers. She could see desire in them. She hoped he couldn't see anything at all in hers.

"Oh, good. You've got a chair, Harry," she said to the little boy and moved to put him in the seat. But Yiannis took him out of her arms and promptly plopped Harry into the chair he'd clamped to the table.

Harry looked startled, then as if remembering what happened when he sat in this chair, he grinned widely and banged his hands vigorously on the table top.

"Where's my grub?" Yiannis said with an indulgent grin. He ruffled Harry's hair, then sat down once more and began to spoon peaches into Harry's mouth.

For a moment Cat could do nothing but watch. And yearn.

"I can do that," she said abruptly. "You can go."

"Here's your hat. What's your hurry? As my grandmother used to say." Yiannis cocked a brow and challenged her with a look.

"I'm sure you're busy, that you have things to do today."

"Yeah." But he didn't stop feeding Harry.

Cat scowled and shifted from one foot to the other. "And I certainly appreciate your taking care of him yesterday and… last night," she added awkwardly. "But I don't want to take any more of your time."

"Don't you?" One dark brow lifted. Another challenge. But she didn't quite understand this one.

"No."

"You're not going to the hospital?"

"Of course I'm going to the hospital. Gran's surgery's at nine. I need to get Harry fed and changed and get on my way—" she glanced at her watch "—soon. Does Harry have a diaper bag?"

"Probably. He's got a load of stuff." Yiannis spooned another mouthful into Harry. "But he can't go with you."

"What? Why not? I'm perfectly capable of taking care of him!" She bristled, indignant that he would imply otherwise just because she'd admitted she didn't have a lot of experience.

"Kids aren't allowed."

She stared. "What?"

"No kids under fourteen. Contagious diseases. Flu, that sort of thing."

"You're joking." But as she said it, she knew he was not. "I didn't realize..."

"Neither did I until they wouldn't let us go up on her floor yesterday."

Cat opened her mouth, then shut it again, confronting the logistics of taking care of Harry and being at the hospital at the same time.

"Harry can stay with me."

"But you—"

The look Yiannis was giving her dared her to argue. Another spoonful went into Harry's mouth. And another.

"I hate to take advantage," she said hesitantly.

Yiannis shrugged, not looking as if he were being taken advantage of at all. "We'll be fine, won't we, buddy?" And the two males grinned at each other. Cat had obviously been left out of the equation entirely.

"Well," she said, "thank you."

Yiannis didn't look at her. "Give her our best." Clearly she'd been dismissed. Yiannis went back to feeding Harry the peaches.

When Cat got to the hospital forty-five minutes later, Gran had already been moved from her bed onto the gurney. She smiled muzzily when Cat came in.

"I feel like something out of the age of Aquarius," Gran mumbled, lifting her hand in greeting but then letting it drop back against the sheet again.

Cat laughed, but couldn't help worrying. Her normally energetic grandmother looked pale and exhausted. Yes, she was probably sedated, and yes, she'd smiled and joked a bit. But Cat's confidence wasn't inspired.

Still she put on her own mental sound recording of "Whistle a Happy Tune" and said determinedly, "You can audition next time they decide to do a production at the musical theater." She reached out and took one of Gran's hands in hers. It was far cooler than usual and her grandmother's skin seemed almost papery when she bent down and kissed her cheek.

Gran smiled and touched Cat's cheek, trailed her fingers along it lightly. Then she shook her head. "I don't think I'll make the chorus line this year," she said wryly. Then she looked past Cat toward the doorway. "Where's Adam?"

"Adam?" Cat blinked in surprise and glanced over her shoulder as if she might see him, which she knew she wouldn't. Gran was not particularly a fan of Adam's, though Cat was at pains to understand why. "At work, I should think."

"He didn't come?"

"You wanted him?" Another surprise.

"Of course not." Gran gave a feeble wave of her hand. "But I thought *you* might."

"I—well, of course, I'd have loved it if Adam could have come. But he can't just take off without warning." Adam's job was demanding and, unlike hers, more than full-time. "Besides I didn't know when I'd get back. I told him I'd call and let him know how it is after you're recovering and I see how you can cope. Which reminds me," she said, fixing her grandmother with a firm look, "when we spoke yesterday, somehow you didn't mention Harry."

"Ah." Gran closed her eyes. "Harry." A slight smile touched her lips.

At the sight of the smile, Cat couldn't keep her mouth shut. "I can't believe you let Misty stick you with him!"

Gran didn't open her eyes. "She's going to talk to Devin."

"So I heard. But that's no excuse."

Her eyes stayed closed, but Gran raised her brows. "Really? I thought it was a pretty good one," she murmured.

Cat ground her teeth. She knew Gran let Misty get away

with plenty, but she didn't think her grandmother actually condoned her behavior. "She takes advantage."

"Well, yes, but it's just—"

"—the way she is, dear," Cat finished for her, still annoyed. It was her grandmother's standard dismissal of inappropriate behavior. "But that doesn't mean it's right."

"I hope you're not intending to take this out on Harry."

"Of course not."

"Or Yiannis?" Gran's eyes opened, clear and blue and sharp. What happened to the age of Aquarius? Or the sedation?

"Yiannis is doing fine. He and Harry are thick as thieves."

Gran smiled. "I thought they would be." She folded her hands just below her breasts and shut her eyes.

"Stop that," Cat said. "You look like a corpse."

Gran laughed. "Not that far gone."

"Good." Cat took both her grandmother's hands and pressed them between hers. "You have to get well," she said urgently, emotions she'd been suppressing threatening to surface all of a sudden. "You're all I've got."

"I thought you had Adam," Gran said. But before Cat could reply that of course she had Adam, that wasn't the same thing, Gran went on. "Where's Harry now?"

"With Yiannis," Cat said stiffly.

"Ah." Gran's lids drifted shut. Her voice grew soft and sleepy again. She smiled, serene and satisfied. "You should marry a man like that."

"Yiannis has no interest in getting married," Cat said sharply.

Gran's eyes snapped open. "You've discussed it?" she demanded.

Cat shrugged dismissively. "It was mentioned in passing."

She had never shared any of her hopes or dreams with her grandmother. Gran knew she and Yiannis had gone out a few times. But after living in the apartment behind him this long, Gran must realize that he had gone out a few times with half the women in Southern California and wasn't interested in a serious relationship.

"Maybe you should discuss it again."

Or maybe not.

"I'll see you in recovery," Cat said, bending to give her grandmother a kiss. "I love you. And I'll be whistling a happy tune for you."

But she wouldn't be talking to Yiannis about marriage. There were some conversations that wouldn't go any better the second time around.

"Family reunion?" Yiannis could feel the word "No," forming on his lips even as he echoed what his mother had just said. But flat-out refusals rarely succeeded with Malena Savas. So he tried hedging. "I'm not sure I can make it."

He held the phone between his ear and his shoulder and bent to reach under the kitchen table and scoop a fast-moving Harry up before the boy could poke his finger into an electrical outlet.

"That's why I'm calling early. To give you plenty of notice. That way you can make sure you have the weekend free." His mother sounded all bright and chipper, but her tone held that be-here-under-pain-of-excommunication edge to it that her children all recognized.

But Yiannis hadn't spent a lifetime perfecting avoidance techniques to let himself be trapped that easily. It wasn't that he didn't like his family. He did—individually. It was that he didn't like crowds. And his family all together "reuniting" was, by any definition, a crowd.

"When is it?"

Having been foiled in his attempt to electrocute himself,

Harry was now trying to poke Yiannis's eyes out. Yiannis batted hands with him, silently. But Harry was giggling.

"Mother's Day weekend," his mother said. "What's that noise?"

"Dish washer."

"It sounds like a child. A baby. Babbling!" Her voice brightened instantly. "Yiannis? Is there something you're not telling me?"

"That I don't know if I can come that weekend."

Malena made an irritated sound. "I picked it specially because your father will be here." Socrates had had a heart attack before Christmas, but he was now back to his full over-worked schedule. Yiannis knew his mother wasn't happy about that, but she'd obviously adjusted. "And," she went on, "so you could all justify coming not just to the reunion but as a way of showing your mother how much you love her."

"Guilt trip in other words."

His mother gave a long-suffering sigh. "If you choose to think of it that way," she said archly.

"I love you."

"Yes, I know. And you hate crowds." She said the words in a sing-song tone that made it clear she'd heard them before—and wasn't buying. "They're not crowds. They're your family."

The crowd you couldn't get rid of, Yiannis thought.

"—and they only want—"

"—what's best for me," Yiannis finished the time-worn aphorism for her. He could have done the sing-song bit, too. It was like a refrain.

"Yes."

"Maybe," he allowed. "But they also want my house during spring break. They want to bring their friends and hang out at the beach all summer. They want me to be the godfather to their children—"

"You should be honored."

"I'm thrilled," he lied through his teeth.

Harry stuck his fingers in Yiannis's mouth, then crowed loudly when Yiannis nibbled on them.

"That's a baby!" Malena announced. "Whose?"

"Not mine," Yiannis said, knowing the jig was up. "Not anyone who's going to make you a grandmother. I've got to go, Ma. Someone's ringing in on my call waiting." It wasn't a lie, actually. There was a call coming in.

"You're trying to get rid of me."

"I'm trying to do business."

"With a baby?"

"Gotta go, Ma. I'll talk to you soon." He hung up before she could have the last word.

But even as he answered the call from a furniture maker in Colorado, he knew he hadn't heard the end of this with his mother. Malena Savas wanted all of her children married and providing her with grandchildren. Now that George and Sophy were back together and expecting a baby any day, he was the last hold-out.

And all his insistence that she should be happy with what she had and stop pressing for what she didn't have fell on deaf ears.

"It isn't for me, Yiannis, darling," she had insisted at Christmas when he'd foolishly gone home and even more foolishly allowed her to corner him in the kitchen the morning he was leaving to have one of her famous heart-to-heart discussions where she told him how he should live his life. "It is for you. It will make you happy! You will be the man you were always meant to be."

"Yeah? Like being married to Dad has made you the happiest woman in the world?"

Every one of the Savas children knew that being married to Socrates Savas was no picnic, just as having him for a father was no walk in the park. He was a hard-working, hard-driving, hard-nosed man.

"Your father is...a challenge," Malena had had the grace to admit. "But he makes life exciting. I wouldn't have the life I have had without him."

"Ain't that the truth," Yiannis had remarked drily.

At which point she had slapped his hand and said firmly, "I love your father, Yiannis, and though he is not always easy, he is always the man I love. I would not change my life for anything on earth."

"That's not because of Dad. It's because of those grandchildren you're finally seeing."

She'd laughed. "Yes, there is that." But then she'd sobered. "Grandchildren are a blessing, Yiannis. I wish them for you—"

"No, thanks. I don't want them."

"But you will."

He'd shaken his head. "I don't intend to."

"We all know where good intentions lead."

"You think not being married is hell?" He'd laughed at that.

"I think you haven't found the right woman yet," his mother told him simply.

Perversely, Yiannis remembered now, a fleeting vision of a red-headed woman with freckles and bottle green eyes had flickered through his mind. Because, Yiannis told himself later, Cat was the one woman who had ever dared mention the M word to him.

"The right woman doesn't exist," he'd told his mother firmly then.

And now, after he finished his conversation with the furniture maker, he sat down on the floor, looked Harry in the eye and said, "No, thanks. I'm single. I'm happy and I'm staying that way."

Harry beamed and waved his hands and climbed into Yiannis's arms.

Just because his mother thought the world was better off with everyone marching through it two by two didn't mean that she was right.

He wasn't going to get married to make his mother happy. Or anyone else. He liked his life just the way it was. He didn't want his freedom compromised. Some people, like Tallie, called him selfish. Maybe he was. But as long as he could remember, families had made demands.

They took your baseball cards, borrowed your surfboard, ate your chocolate Easter egg, spilled red wine on the sport coat you were nice enough to lend them. Mostly they made demands on your time.

Hell, they were still doing it.

A family reunion on Mother's Day, for crying out loud.

"Don't get married," he told Harry sternly. "No matter what they tell you."

Harry poked him in the eye.

Cat didn't know much about relativity.

A liberal arts sort of girl, she'd taken high school physics and nothing much scientific since.

But it didn't need an advanced degree to convince her that time was relative. And she was never more certain of it than while she alternately sat and paced around the surgical waiting room.

Waiting was the operative word.

And there was a pun for you, she thought with annoyance. How on earth long could it take?

"I will come and speak to you after," Dr Singh had told her, giving her an encouraging smile outside the operating room. But she could tell from his eyes he was already mentally somewhere else.

She hoped the somewhere else was the operating room because three hours later he was still apparently replacing her grandmother's hip.

Other people had been called in to talk to the doctor about their patient. A number had come and sat and waited and were now long gone again. All of them seemed to be there in groups. To have support.

Not Cat. Cat paced alone up and down the corridor and cracked her knuckles. She bit her fingernails and said her prayers.

When finally her mobile phone rang—they would call when the doctor could see her, she'd been told—she snatched it up. "Yes?"

"Hi." It was Adam.

Cat felt the air seem to seep right out of her. "Hi." The single word came out wobbly-sounding.

"Tired?" Adam said. "I told you not to drive down last night."

"I had to," Cat told him, just as she had yesterday before she'd left. "Gran's in surgery now. She should be out soon."

"Great. So are you coming back tonight then?"

"What? No!"

"Well, when are you coming back?" he asked, as if it were a perfectly reasonable question.

"I don't know." Cat flexed her shoulders which felt suddenly stiff. "I just got here. I don't know how she is. Or how long she'll be in the hospital."

"Well, you can't do anything for her if she's there," Adam said. "And you can't take days and days off. People are counting on you."

"I'm a substitute librarian," Cat said. "And my grandmother is counting on me as well."

"Of course," Adam said placatingly. "I was just saying."

"Thank you for saying," Cat said, annoyed.

"I miss you."

"Oh." Her annoyance abated a bit. She smiled. "I miss you, too."

"And what about your dress?"

"What dress?"

"The dress you have to get for the Wanamakers' ball." The CEO of Adam's bank held a ball once a year. It was an exclusive affair, and you had to be Someone to get invited. Last year was the first year Adam had been invited. Last year she hadn't gone with him—they hadn't been engaged then. They had only met a month or so before. But, eyes shining, he had told her all about it.

When they got engaged in January, one of the first things he had said to her was, "This year you can go to Wanamakers' with me."

Now he said, "You're not going to let me down, are you, Cat?"

"Of course not! I would never!" But she hadn't given it a thought when she'd made her decision to come.

"It's only a week from Saturday night and you still don't have a dress." He sounded distinctly worried.

Most men would assume that the woman they had chosen to ask to such an event would be capable of picking out a suitable dress. Not Adam.

"You have to look elegant," he'd told her when he'd showed her the invitation. And there had been a note of doubt in his voice when they'd talked about the dress. His gaze had skated slowly up and down the gypsy skirt and gauzy blouse she'd worn to work at the library, and his expression had seemed to suggest that he wondered if that was even possible.

"Absolutely," Cat had vowed. "It'll be an excuse to buy a new dress," she had added with more enthusiasm than she felt.

"I'll go with you."

And no amount of discussion had convinced him otherwise. So far, though, they hadn't gone. Not that he hadn't suggested it.

But every time she hadn't been able to go. Just as well, she'd assured herself. She didn't want Adam breathing down her neck while she went dress shopping. She didn't like shopping for dresses at the best of times.

Ever since eighth grade when she'd overheard Michael Garner say she looked like a knock-kneed crane, Cat had had issues with her body. She didn't like looking at her crane-ish self in mirrors, let alone in triple mirrors where she appeared in infinitely disastrous multiplication.

She'd get a dress, but by herself. And it would be one she felt good in. She'd make a stab at "elegance," but she considered it a bonus.

Suddenly there was an up-side to dear Gran's broken hip.

"There are dresses down here," she told Adam now. "I'll look."

There was a long pause. Then Adam said, "I suppose you'll have to. You can't let this go until you get back. But remember: elegant." And he added, "And not black."

"Why not?" When she heard the word "elegant" Cat thought only of black.

It was hard enough not to stand out when you were nearly six feet tall, had hair that might not be the color of a fire engine, but certainly called one to mind. Anything other than black had never crossed her mind.

"Because it's not a funeral," Adam said. "It's a joyous occasion."

Cat thought it was a duty function. "I'll look at colors," she promised. She didn't say she would buy one.

"I'll call you tonight to see what you've found."

"I may not go this afternoon, Adam."

"Why not?"

"Because Gran is in surgery!"

"Oh, right. Of course. Well, keep me posted. I have a meeting now. I'll talk to you later. Love you."

"You, too," Cat said, but Adam had already hung up.

She got a cup of coffee from the urn by the desk and stirred it absently as she paced the floor. Her stomach was in tighter knots now, as much from the thought of dress shopping as from worrying about Gran. The strong bitter taste of the coffee made her wince.

"She still in surgery?"

Cat nearly dropped the mug. She spun around. Yiannis, with Harry on his hip, was standing right behind her.

"What are you doing here?" she demanded.

"I thought you'd call when she got out of surgery. You didn't, so we came to see how she was doing. How are *you* doing?" he asked, as if that were more important.

"I'm all right," she said, aware that she didn't sound it. "I didn't call because they haven't called me. I don't know what's going on. And I thought you couldn't bring babies to the hospital."

"He can't go to her room. He can stay here. So we're here." The look he gave her defied her to argue. "Are you that upset?"

Cat swallowed. "I'm all right. It just seems as if it's taking forever."

"Yeah, it did when my dad had his heart surgery."

She hadn't heard about that. But he didn't elaborate. He just asked, "When did she go in? How long did they say it would take?"

So Cat found herself telling him. It felt good to be able to talk to someone who cared about Gran, even if it was Yiannis. They walked down the hall and back into the waiting room. While she talked, Yiannis poured himself a cup of coffee and, without even asking, took hers out of her hand and refilled it. She hadn't even realized she'd drained it.

He handed her a full cup.

"Thank you." She wrapped her hands around the mug and breathed deeply, feeling steadier. She managed a smile.

"Good," Yiannis said abruptly.

Cat blinked at him. "Good?"

"First time you've smiled all day." He regarded her solemnly over the top of his coffee mug. She remembered other times when he'd looked at her that way, his gaze warm, caring.

"Ms. MacLean?"

Jolted, Cat turned to see Dr Singh just coming in the waiting room, his eyes finding her. So much for phone call warnings. "I'm Catriona MacLean," she said. "Is my grandmother all right?"

The doctor nodded and tipped his head toward one of the small conference rooms just off the main waiting room. "She will be."

Cat tried to read his expression, but he had one of those inscrutable faces. Why didn't they teach doctors to smile?

"If you and your husband will come this way," he said politely. "I will explain things to you."

Husband?

She expected an instant denial from Yiannis, but he just said, "Do you want to go in alone? Harry and I can wait out here."

"No." She'd felt alone all morning. It might be the height of folly to allow even for a moment the misconception that Yiannis was her husband, but as long as they both knew it wasn't true, what difference would it make to the doctor?

Dr Singh led them into a small conference room where he waited until she sat down before he sat, too. Yiannis didn't sit. He stood behind her, jiggling Harry, keeping the baby entertained as the doctor spread out several sheets of paper on the desk between them.

"Your grandmother is doing very well," he said. "She is in recovery now, and we'll keep her there for a while. We need to be cautious because of her age. But when she is ready to go back to her room, you can go back with her. Not the baby," he said apologetically.

"We understand," Cat said quickly.

Dr Singh smiled perfunctorily, then pushed one of the illustrations toward her. "With the sort of break she had, we did a replacement. It will be more stable in the long run. You see?" But she noted that he wasn't talking to her. He was talking to Yiannis.

Cat bristled.

"Are those illustrations?" Yiannis asked. His hand came past her shoulder as he gestured at the pieces of paper the doctor had laid on the table.

"Yes. I will show you what we did." He talked—at length—but for all that she tried to focus, Cat wasn't absorbing it.

She didn't speak medical jargon. But even more importantly, she couldn't seem to focus on the pages when she was so aware of the man literally breathing down her neck. She tried to follow the doctor's pen as he drew a line and a circle and explained what each symbolized. But even then, she was far more attuned to the movement of Yiannis's feet as he shifted behind her, to the timbre of his voice as he asked questions, to his request for amplification when something wasn't clear. Out of the corner of her eye she could see the faded denim of his jeans, could watch the muscles shift beneath the fabric as he moved.

"—any other questions?" The doctor's voice cut across her thought. "Ms MacLean."

"What? Oh!" Cat was suddenly aware of Dr Singh looking at her expectantly.

"When can she come home?" Yiannis asked.

"She'll be out-patient in three or four days. We'll see how she does. But she won't be going home for a while. She'll need some time for rehab in-patient first. And then she'll have to do out-patient therapy. It's a several weeks' process."

Exactly what Cat was afraid of.

"She won't like that," Yiannis predicted.

The doctor smiled. "Probably not. But it's necessary if she's going to get back on her feet again."

"She will," Yiannis said. "She lives in a second floor apartment."

The doctor winced. "Not right away, she doesn't. You'll have to find somewhere else." He gathered up the papers, slipped them into a folder and handed them to Cat, then stood up. "But it will give her a greater incentive. I'll be talking to her about it tomorrow when she's able to focus on what I'm telling her. If either of you can be here, it would be a good idea."

"Of course," Yiannis said.

Numbly Cat nodded her head and stood, too.

Dr Singh shook Yiannis's hand, then Cat's. "Don't worry," he said to both of them. "She'll do fine. She's got a lot of drive. And she has a family who cares about her. That's important. The receptionist will let you know when they've taken her to her room and you can see her there. Minus your little boy." He gave Harry a wink and tousled his hair, then strode back out the door, leaving Cat standing there with Yiannis and Harry and the sense that her life was spinning out of control.

"She can't go home," Cat said. Of course she should have realized it. The minute her grandmother had said the hip was broken, at some point she'd known. But she'd been so busy worrying about the long run—what she would do if Gran wasn't able to live alone anymore—that she hadn't considered the short term.

"Not right away," Yiannis agreed.

"I'll have to move her to San Francisco." Cat said, thinking aloud, trying to figure things out because Gran wouldn't be able to live with her there, either. She lived in a third floor walk-up herself. Maybe she could find a short-term studio apartment lease. Or an assisted living place or—

"Why?" Yiannis's question broke into her darting thoughts.

"Because she can't climb stairs! Weren't you listening?"

Yiannis swung Harry up onto his shoulders and gave her a long-suffering look. "I was listening, but I didn't hear him say anything about her having to move to San Francisco. There are street level accommodations on the island."

"They'll cost a mint." Balboa was a tourist destination. A summer holiday mecca of note.

"She's already paying rent," Yiannis said mildly.

"Exactly. Stupidest thing she ever did, selling her house." Cat glared at him, even though logically it wasn't his fault.

"Relax," Yiannis said easily, which infuriated her. Then he nettled her further by taking her elbow and steering her out of the little room and past the receptionist toward the corridor. He smiled at the receptionist as they passed.

Cat sputtered. "Easy for you to say. She's not your problem." They were in the corridor now and she stopped and pulled her arm away.

"She's not a problem at all. She can stay with me."

Cat stared. "What?"

He shrugged. "I have two steps up to the door. She can do those or I can make a ramp. And I have a spare bedroom—" the recollection of which seemed to provoke a sudden grimace "—and she's welcome to it." His grimace faded at those words.

"She won't—" Cat began, then stopped. She had been going to say that Gran would never go along with the notion, but a moment's reflection told her that her grandmother was more likely to agree to staying with Yiannis than moving to San Francisco.

"She will," Yiannis said confidently, "as long as you don't throw a fit."

"Me?" Cat bristled. "Why would I throw a fit?"

His brows lifted. His eyes challenged her. "Couldn't say." His tone was mild. "But in case you were considering it, have second thoughts."

Cat gave him a level stare which he met with an equally steady one of his own. She was the one who looked away first. "We'll see," she muttered. "There are, as you say, options."

"Yes, but Maggie will be upset if it's up in the air."

Annoyed, Cat knew he was right. But she didn't have to like it. "We aren't saying anything for the moment," she told him firmly. "When she's awake and aware and we know what she's up against, there will be time enough to make a decision then."

"If you say so."

"I say so." Cat was firm. "And why did you let the doctor think you were my husband?"

He shrugged. "What difference does it make? He didn't care. Unless maybe you were angling for a date with him?" He cocked his head and gave her a speculative look.

"I was not angling for a date! I'm engaged!"

"So I heard. When's he coming down?"

As if it were a requirement of her fiancé to be here. "He's very busy."

The look Yiannis gave her said he didn't think Adam ought to be too busy to come. Fortunately he didn't give voice to the thought. He only said, "That's what Maggie says."

So Gran had told him about Adam. "What else did she say?"

"Not a lot." He winced when Harry grabbed handfuls of his hair and bounced on his shoulders. Then he glanced at his watch. "You don't need me to stay until the receptionist calls you?"

"Of course not."

The mouth twisted again. "Didn't think so. Okay. Harry and I'll head home. Tell Maggie I came by, and that I'll be by sometime tomorrow. Give me a call when you're leaving this afternoon. I'll get dinner ready."

"Dinner?" she echoed doubtfully. "You don't have to—"

"I know I don't. But I want some time to work this evening. So after you see Maggie come back and take care of Harry. I'll have dinner ready."

He wasn't offering. He was commanding. And the point of the exercise was to be sure she was there to take care of Harry. She nodded. "Fine. Thank you," she said stiffly. "I appreciate it."

He nodded, satisfied. Then he slid Harry off his shoulders. "Give your aunt Cat a kiss good-bye."

Cat's eyes widened in surprise. But Harry apparently understood more than she had given him credit for. He held out his arms to her and pursed his lips. And as amazed as she was, Cat felt something tender and maternal squeeze in the vicinity of her heart.

Smiling, she leaned in and touched her lips to Harry's. Then she kissed his cheek and the tip of his nose for good measure before stepping back again—only to be shocked as she found herself kissed again.

By Yiannis.

Not a swept-off-your-feet kiss. Not a passionate exploration of mutual attraction. Not a long kiss at all.

But stunning in its unexpectedness—and in her gut reaction. If Harry's pursed lips brought sensation to the general region of her heart, Yiannis's arrowed straight home. Their touch brought with it such myriad sensations and emotions that she backed up a step to stand against the wall, her fingers curling into fists and pressing against it so she wouldn't reach up and loop her arms around his neck and make it longer, harder, deeper.

And then, in a moment—barely more—he'd stepped away again, smiling. Something unreadable flashed in his gaze. Cat felt her lips tingle and her face flame.

"What was that for?" she demanded indignantly.

Yiannis nodded past her toward the waiting room from which they'd come. "She looked like she was expecting it."

"What? Who?" Cat's head whipped around and she saw the receptionist suddenly busy herself with paperwork on her desk. "You kissed me because a receptionist expected it?"

Yiannis shook his head, still smiling. "Nope. I kissed you because I wanted to." And he ducked in and gave her another for good measure, then slung Harry up on his shoulders again. "See you at dinner."

CHAPTER FOUR

HE WAS out of his mind.

Kissing Cat MacLean? *Twice?*

Yiannis's fingers tightened on the steering wheel and he shook his head at his own stupidity. What the hell had he been thinking?

Well, he hadn't been. Or not with his brain, anyway. Other parts of his anatomy had always spoken a lot louder whenever he was around Cat. From the minute he'd seen her in front of her grandmother's house with her arms full of grocery bags, he'd wanted her. And as he got to know her, the more time he'd spent with her—in bed and out—nothing had changed.

Only Cat had changed things when after the best three months of his life, she'd demanded to know where she stood.

He hadn't seen what was wrong with the status quo. They had great conversation, energetic arguments, lots of fun and the best sex he could ever remember.

Why wasn't that enough?

She hadn't given him a satisfactory answer. She'd only made it clear that she wanted more—marriage, kids, picket fences.

Encumbrances. Duties. Responsibilities. Yiannis knew the drill.

But Cat hadn't seen it that way—and obviously still didn't

if that honking great engagement ring on her finger was anything to go by.

Still, where was Mr Fiancé now when she needed him?

Busy, to hear Cat tell it.

Didn't make sense to Yiannis. How could he be too busy to show up and hold her hand through Maggie's surgery? Didn't he know how much Cat's grandmother meant to her?

Yiannis damned well knew.

And when she didn't call and didn't call and didn't call, he did his own share of pacing. And as soon as Harry was up from his nap, he'd bundled the little boy into his car seat and headed for the hospital.

Good thing he had. One look at Cat's tense shoulders as she'd stared out the window and he knew she was shouldering far too much alone. She needed someone with her. Then she'd needed someone to ask questions when the doctor finally showed up. And after he'd left, she'd needed someone to assure her she wasn't going to have to take Maggie off to San Francisco which, if she'd been thinking straight, Cat would know Maggie would hate.

And then she'd needed someone to kiss her.

And he was there, wasn't he? The useless fiancé could have done it if he'd been here. But he wasn't. So Yiannis had done it for him.

But mostly he'd done it because, like he'd told her, he'd wanted to.

He supposed he ought to resist. He didn't ordinarily hit on engaged women. But this was different. This was Cat.

When had he ever resisted Cat?

Well, he hadn't. It was marriage he'd resisted, not her.

Where Cat was concerned, the same attraction was still there. He felt the same quickening of his pulse, the same tightening of his body. And he could still taste her now if he ran his tongue over his lips.

He reconsidered those kisses.

He should have taken his time.

Cat refused to think about Yiannis kissing her.

She'd scrubbed them away with the back of her hand the minute he left the room. She didn't know what he thought he was doing. But his kisses were pointless. Meaningless. Annoying. Irritating. Vexing.

And the effect they had on her rocked her to her toes.

They would have rattled her peace of mind all by themselves if the sight of Gran hadn't done it immediately thereafter.

If Gran had looked frail yesterday, it was nothing to the woman Cat beheld when she walked into her grandmother's hospital room after the surgery. Granted, Gran was not a big woman, but she looked positively tiny engulfed in the big white bed. Her eyes were closed, her lips pale, and her cheeks almost the same color as the sheet that covered her.

Cat halted abruptly just inside the door, her fingers knotting together as she took a deep breath and tried to get her bearings. She had to reassure herself so she could do the same for her grandmother when she woke. But the only thing that gave her any hope right now was the green line that jumped across the black screen, proving that her grandmother still had a heart beat.

"She's doing very well." The nurse swooped past her to come into the room, making notes on what she read on the machines.

"Who's doing well?" A faint raspy voice disputed from the bed.

"Gran!" Cat flew across the room to see her grandmother's eyes flutter open and a slight smile touch her lips.

"I'm still here," Gran said, sounding grumpy.

"Of course you are," Cat said fervently as she took Gran's

hand and pressed it to her lips. It was cool, but Gran's fingers wrapped hers and gave a reassuring squeeze. "And thank God for that."

"You may not be by the time I get home," Gran said. Her voice was more gravelly than usual.

"Oh, yes I will," Cat vowed. She bent and kissed Gran's cheek, too, glad to discover it felt a bit warmer even as her grandmother's eyes fluttered shut.

The nurse took Gran's vitals, then turned to Cat. "You can stay if you want but she'll mostly sleep."

Gran's eyes opened. "No, she can't stay. She needs to go home. You need to help Yiannis with Harry."

"Yiannis is doing quite well without me," Cat admitted. "He and Harry came by while you were in surgery."

Gran smiled sleepily. "He's a good boy."

He? Harry? Or Yiannis?

Unsure, Cat didn't respond.

"Go home," Gran urged.

Cat shook her head. "Not yet."

"Are you worrying about me?" Gran's eyes were accusing.

"I—a little," Cat admitted because there had never been any future in lying to her grandmother. "But I'm whistling a happy tune," she added with a bright smile.

Gran gave a small chuckle. "I should think you'd be wishing me over the rainbow."

"Never!"

Gran's fingers plucked at the sheet. "There will come a time."

"No."

"I'm complicating your life."

"You're part of my life," Cat said firmly. "One of the very best parts."

"I'm glad you think so," Gran said simply, then shook her

head. "You'll probably change your mind when I get out of here. When do I get out of here?"

"I don't know yet," Cat said honestly. "You have a couple more days in the hospital. Then you'll do in-patient rehab. Dr Singh said he'd come talk to you tomorrow morning."

She didn't mention Yiannis's offer. Not now. Not yet. Hopefully not ever. Maybe Gran would realize it was a bad idea to try to ever move back into the apartment over the garage and would suggest that she come to San Francisco to be near Cat.

As if her thoughts had prompted it, her mobile phone rang.

"It's Adam," Cat told Gran and then said into the phone, "Hi. Perfect timing. Gran's out of surgery. Doing well."

"Great. And I solved your dress problem."

"You— What?"

"I had lunch today with Margarita at Lolo's," he reported. "You remember her."

Cat did. Margarita was a young woman on the fast track that he worked with. Margarita was svelte, sophisticated and smart. Whenever she was around Margarita, songs about not measuring up played in Cat's head.

"I told her you needed a dress for the ball," Adam went on. "And she said she knew the perfect place to look. Trendy, sophisticated. Elegant."

There was that word again. "I can get my own dress, Adam. There are plenty of places down here to look."

"Sure. But I thought you'd be spending all your time at the hospital. I didn't want you to feel pressured. Margarita said she'd be happy to pick one for you."

Cat knew he was only trying to be helpful. She took a careful breath, aware that even though Gran's eyes were closed, her ears were not. She would be hearing one side of the conversation—and coming to conclusions.

"I'm sure I can manage," Cat said evenly and with all the

equanimity she could muster. "But please thank Margarita for me."

"If you're sure," Adam began reluctantly.

"If I run into problems, I'll let you know."

"Please do," Adam said. "If you haven't found it by the weekend, and you still can't come home, I'll come down and help you."

"Would you?" Suddenly having him here seemed like a very good idea. There would be no time to think about annoying meaningless kisses from Yiannis if Adam was here.

"I'll see what I can do. I'll give you a call tomorrow. Give your grandmother my best. Love you."

"Love you, too," Cat said. She closed her phone slowly, trying to hang onto the satisfactory bits of the conversation, trying to muster a vision of Adam's blond good looks and smooth handsome face.

Adam Collier was a stunningly good looking man, his features far more conventionally handsome than Yiannis's. But once she made the mental comparison, it was Yiannis's face who kept intruding in her thoughts. Maybe because Gran was talking about Yiannis again.

"It's lovely of him to take care of Harry."

"Yes."

"He's been such a help since he moved in. Selling the house to him was the best thing I've done in years."

Maybe not, Cat wanted to say. Not now you can't climb stairs. But saying that would open a can of worms she didn't want to deal with tonight.

Gran shut her eyes and sighed, then opened them again just slightly. "I had hoped you and Yiannis might…get together?" It was the first time she'd ever said that. Perhaps not the first time she'd thought it, but she'd never given voice to the hope before.

"No," Cat said firmly.

Gran sighed. She shook her head wearily. "Well, of course, I was only hoping. Don't you like him?"

Cat smiled politely. "He's been very good to you."

"Yes, but I meant you—"

"Yiannis doesn't do the long haul."

"Maybe he just needs a reason," Gran suggested, a smile flickering on her lips.

Cat didn't respond. "Life is not a fairy tale," she said at last. "Or a Broadway musical."

Gran reached out and took her hand, chafing it lightly between her own. "Sadly, you're right. But you must admit, those songs do have their uses."

"They do."

But there were limits. She stood up and bent to give her grandmother a kiss. "I've got to go. Yiannis has had Harry all day. It's time I took over."

Gran smiled. "You're a dear girl."

"Of course I am." Cat smiled.

"Yiannis should see that."

"Adam sees it," Cat said firmly.

Gran raised her brows. "I sincerely hope so."

She should have said no to dinner.

Even if she made sure that Yiannis didn't know he could still affect her, dinner with him, even chaperoned by a bouncing baby, was exactly what she did not need.

It was like dancing with the devil. Far too appealing, much too tempting. And even being engaged to Adam sadly didn't seem to make her impervious to Yiannis's charms.

And the truly dismaying thing was that he wasn't even trying. He was just being himself—the man she'd fallen in love with three years ago.

Why couldn't he be rude or dismissive or obnoxious? It

would be so much easier to ignore him. It was mortifying to find herself still so aware of him.

And she didn't need more mortification where Yiannis was concerned.

Maybe she could plead a headache, just pick up Harry and run—well, walk, really—to Gran's and eat whatever Gran had in her refrigerator.

Yes, that would work. There was no sense subjecting herself to a one-on-one with a man who undermined her best resolutions to mentally put him in a no-look, no-touch, no-fanciful dreams box and shut the door.

One more deep breath to fortify herself and she got out of the car, marched through the gate and went round to the back door where she knocked briskly, then tried to look as if she really did have a headache when Yiannis opened it.

But when the door opened it wasn't Yiannis standing there.

It was another gorgeous man, a little taller than Yiannis, a little younger, his lean frame still a bit coltish, probably about her age—twenty-six. His black hair was damp, his smile was stunning, his chest was bare, his hips were clad in a pair of low-slung board shorts. His grey-green eyes studied her appreciatively as the smile broadened.

"You must be Cat," he said, opening the door wider and drawing her in with the mere force of his personality. "Come on in. I'm Milos. Savas," he added.

Not that she'd had any doubt. The resemblance was striking.

"Yian's cousin," he said, shaking her hand warmly and not letting go. In fact he was drawing her right into the kitchen. "Yiannis is changing the kid. You're Harry's aunt?"

"Er, yes. Sort of." Perhaps not legally, but certainly in terms of how she perceived family. "His mother is my cousin. Sort of."

Milos just grinned and nodded. "Yeah, families are like

that. How about a beer? Or—" he opened the refrigerator and peered in "—iced tea? I'm sure he's got wine somewhere."

"Iced tea," Cat said, and as soon as she had, realized that she'd lost the opportunity to plead a headache.

Milos poured her a glass of tea, handed it to her, then popped the cap on a bottle of beer for himself. "Want a beer, Yian?" he yelled.

There was no immediate answer. But seconds later Yiannis ambled into the room with Harry on one arm. He'd obviously been to the beach. He still wore a pair of board shorts and a T-shirt with the neck torn out and his hair was damp and spiky. Cat's traitorous heart kicked into double-time.

"You've met Milos," he said gruffly.

"I have," Cat agreed. "I'm sorry. I would have picked Harry up sooner, but I didn't realize you were having company."

"Neither did I."

"Hey." Milos grinned. "Neely rang you to say I was coming."

"Which doesn't constitute an invitation," Yiannis pointed out.

Milos shrugged unrepentantly. "You can come and stay with me," he offered, opening a second beer and handing it to Yiannis.

"On some god-forsaken coral atoll. Not likely."

Cat listened to the grumbled exchange enviously. With no siblings—and no cousins except the difficult Misty—she was enchanted by all such conversations.

Yiannis, however, abruptly changed the subject. "How's Maggie?"

"Um…doing well," Cat said, trying to drag her attention back to that. "So they say at least," she added. "She looks very pale. Very…small. I've never thought of Gran as small."

"I have," Yiannis said. But then he was a good eight inches taller and seventy pounds heavier than Gran who barely topped one hundred pounds fully dressed. Plus, he'd never known the truly strong and powerful woman Gran had once been. "But I know what you mean," he went on. "She seems bigger than she is. She's a force."

So maybe he did have some notion of the real Gran. Cat nodded. "Yes."

"Sorry I didn't get to meet her," Milos said. "And I probably won't as I'm just here for a few days."

"Not few enough," Yiannis muttered as he tipped the drink to his lips.

Milos grinned. "He's just mad because he didn't get the phone message that I was coming. He doesn't get any hospitality awards."

"Because I'm not hospitable."

"His mother is. She told Seb and Neely—that's my brother and sister-in-law," he explained for Cat's benefit, "that Yian would be glad to have me stay with him when I was passing through. I'm on my way to the South Pacific," he explained to Cat. "Two years working in a clinic on one of the islands."

"He's a quack," Yiannis said.

"I'm a doctor. Just finished my ENT residency."

Cat's eyes widened. A doctor? He looked about eighteen.

"You don't have to be impressed," Yiannis said. "He's going so he can bask in the sun, go surfing and pick up girls."

"That, too," Milos said, unoffended. "He's just jealous because he didn't think of it."

"I puked dissecting a frog." Yiannis was matter-of-fact. "Put an end to all my medical aspirations. Here, hold Harry while I put on the steaks."

And before Cat could respond, she had Harry deposited in her arms and Yiannis was opening the refrigerator. Harry looked instantly doubtful. But when Cat managed a genuine grin and began to talk to him, his expression cleared.

She was sure that hers did, too. She'd have been mortified

if he'd burst into tears. In fact, he seemed to like her. At least he twisted in her arms and patted her cheek and said something in babyese to her.

"What's that?" she asked him.

"He wants to go outside and watch the steaks grill," Yiannis said. "Come on." And he shouldered open the door and carried a plateful of steak outside to where he already had a fire going on a small grill. He was holding the door for her, waiting. So Cat tried to edge through it, Harry on her hip and the glass of iced tea in her hand. She was careful to keep her distance, but she couldn't help remembering when they had been dating and she hadn't hesitated to brush against him.

"I'll hold the door," Milos said and pushed it open further so that Yiannis could move on and she could get out more easily.

"Thank you. I should just go on home," she said when she got out there. "You have company and Harry and I will be fine."

"I bought you a steak," Yiannis said flatly. He was slapping three on the grill even as he spoke and, of course, once he had, she couldn't politely beg off. Thank God, and Yiannis's mother, that Milos was there.

They were going to eat at a table on the brick patio between Yiannis's house and the garage and Gran's apartment. The small garden was full of Gran's flowers and greenery and reminded Cat of all the years she had spent playing right here under the watchful eye of her grandmother. Now it was she who watched as Harry crawled about and put things in his mouth.

"Oh, Harry! Don't!" she exclaimed and removed first a twig and then a stone and then wood shavings undoubtedly left from some building project of Yiannis's. She scooped Harry up and distracted him, playing pat-a-cake, and trying not to let her gaze fasten on the man who was grilling steaks across the patio.

Milos set the table and chatted with her, asking about her work in San Francisco, drawing her out about the fabric puppets she made and the fabric art pieces she also sold. Yiannis didn't say a word, but she suspected he was listening so she made it clear how happy she was there. Then she asked Milos about why he had really applied at the clinic, where the island was, where he'd gone to medical school, what had made him decide to specialize in ear, nose and throat issues.

Neither of them included Yiannis in the conversation. He could participate if he wanted. He wasn't shy, so Cat figured he'd include himself.

But he didn't. She caught him watching her when she glanced his way. But he didn't speak, just focused on the grill.

When the steaks and corn on the cob were ready, he went into the house and brought out deli cartons of coleslaw and potato salad, then went up to Gran's and brought down Harry's portable collapsible chair.

"I'm sorry. I could have done that," Cat said.

He shrugged. "You had your hands full." He attached it to the picnic table, then scooped Harry up off the patio and plopped him in. "Let's eat."

They ate. Milos talked. Harry smeared butter in his hair. And Cat sat across the table from Yiannis and remembered the last time she'd sat here.

They'd eaten dinner with Gran. Yiannis had grilled salmon that night. And when they'd dished up the meal, he'd sat down across from her and slid a bare foot beneath the table and run it up her calf. Cat had jumped, then blushed furiously.

"Something bite you?" Gran asked.

"N-no. I mean, yes."

Yiannis had grinned and talked easily to Gran just as if he hadn't been seducing her granddaughter right before her eyes. And Cat had gone to her seduction willingly. No, eagerly.

Gran had gone up to her apartment after the meal, but Cat had lingered. "To help Yiannis with the dishes," she'd said. "Then maybe go for a walk."

Gran was no fool. She had seen the smouldering looks that had passed between Cat and Yiannis, but she hadn't grabbed Cat by the arm and said, "No! You're coming with me!"

Of course Cat had been an adult. And Gran had never been the sort of person who commandeered.

It might have been better if she had been, Cat thought now. But she didn't blame Gran for her own mistake. She knew better now. She wouldn't make the same mistake again.

She stole a glance at Yiannis and found him watching her. Quickly she averted her gaze and tucked her legs under her in her chair. Then she turned to Milos and began asking about his time in med school.

Milos was happy to talk. He lazed back in his chair, sipping his beer, his hooded gaze never wavering from her as he answered her questions. He was obviously happy to bask in her attention. And if he wondered why she never turned her gaze on Yiannis, he didn't make any effort to include his cousin, either.

For his part, Yiannis might as well not have been there. He ate stolidly through his meal without saying a thing.

The sun dropped lower in the sky. The garden was totally in shadows now, hiding Yiannis's expression and the direction of his gaze. But Cat didn't need to see it to feel his eyes on her. Every time she glanced his way now, though, he was forking another bite of steak into his mouth or making faces at Harry who was giggling and eating bits of finger food that Cat had set out for him.

Maybe it was just her imagination making her the center

of his attention. Surely he wasn't interested. He knew what she wanted—and she knew what he didn't want.

Doubtless he had had plenty of women since she'd moved away. He probably even had one—or more—in his life now.

And she had a man in hers. The right man.

She rubbed her thumb over her ring, and Milos said, "Heck of a stone. Mean something?" His grin glinted in the light above the door.

So she told him about Adam. She tried not to lay it on too thick, but she felt she needed to make sure Yiannis knew she was in love with another man.

Milos listened politely, then grinned and said, "He's not here, though, is he?"

Cat blinked, then tapped her heart. "He's here."

Milos nodded, then stretched his arms over his head. "You're welcome to bring him along then."

"What?"

"I thought we could go out for a while. There has to be some night life hereabouts." He looked inquiringly at Yiannis who gave a wordless shrug.

Milos looked at him for a long moment, then pushed himself forward to sit on the end of the chaise, ready to move. "Of course there is," he went on confidently and stood up. He looked down at Cat.

"Come with me," he invited. "Save me from the unattached women of Balboa Island. Yian can watch the kid."

"Thanks," she said, "but I need to take care of Harry."

"Yiannis is a great babysitter," Milos insisted. "He babysat me."

"Still am," Yiannis said.

Milos laughed, but his gaze stayed on Cat. "You sure…?" He let his voice trail off enticingly.

Cat nodded, not even glancing at Yiannis. "Very sure. But thank you."

"Too bad," Milos said as he gathered up plates and condiments and prepared to carry them into the house. Cat got to her feet, too, and began cleaning up the rest of the things on the table.

"Thank you for dinner. I need to get Harry up to bed, but I'll help with the dishes first." They were the first words she'd spoken to Yiannis since before dinner.

He looked up at her, then slowly stood. Cat felt her breath catch as their gazes locked. "Leave them," he said. "Harry needs to go to sleep." As he spoke, his eyes left hers and he unstrapped the little boy from the chair, swung him out into his arms, then carried him into the house where he washed Harry's very messy face and hands and hair.

Cat followed silently with the last of the dishes.

"Put them on the table. I'll take care of them," Yiannis instructed as he dried Harry's hands and face, then tickled his belly and made faces at him for a moment, saying, "See you tomorrow, buddy." There was a pause. Then abruptly he thrust the little boy into Cat's arms. "Good night."

He couldn't have made her dismissal any more clear if he had opened the door and held it for her—which moments later he did.

Cat clutched Harry so tightly that he squirmed and let out a yelp of protest. Feeling foolish, she loosened her grip.

"Good night, then," she said tersely and walked past him without a glance. She didn't need a glance. He was so close that she could feel the heat from his body as she passed.

"Thank you for the dinner," she added. No one was going to say she'd forgotten her manners.

She was halfway across the patio when the screen door banged shut behind her and she heard Yiannis yell at Milos, "We can go to Tino's if you want to meet women."

* * *

Tino's was hopping.

Even on a week night, the noise was deafening, the bodies were pressed close, and the drinks were flowing freely. Milos plunged into the crowd, heading toward the bar. "I'll buy the beers," he called over his shoulder.

Yiannis let him, choosing to lean against the stucco wall just outside the door. He shoved his hands into the pockets of his jeans. There had been a time when he'd first come to Balboa, that Yiannis had spent nearly every evening at Tino's or one of the other local watering holes.

Now, as he finally stepped inside the room, he wondered if he would even stay until Milos got back with the beers. He looked around at the girls on the make and the guys on the prowl and knew why he spent most of his evenings now hard at work in his shop sanding and sawing and refinishing furniture. He felt old.

Also annoyed. As he watched Milos, beers in his hands, stop working his way back across the room to chat up a pretty young thing who looked barely older than Harry, Yiannis ground his teeth.

Not because of the girl. Hell, Milos could have the girl.

His annoyance was that Milos was here at all. He'd been grinding his teeth since he had opened the door this afternoon to find his cousin standing on his doorstep.

"Hey," Milos had said. "Remember me?"

Yiannis wished he could say no.

"Aunt Malena said she sent an email," Milos had offered when Yiannis hadn't immediately drawn him in. Then when Yiannis still didn't open the door any wider, Milos had sagged a bit, then rubbed a hand over his rumpled hair. "I suppose I could sleep on a street corner."

Yiannis had been tempted to let him. It wasn't that he begrudged his cousin a place to sleep. It was the unspoken assumption made by everyone in his family that they could drop in whenever they wanted with no thought to what he wanted. It was why he had had enough of family. Why he didn't need any more of them messing up his life.

Besides, tonight he'd had other plans.

He'd been going to have dinner with Cat.

They'd had dinner together, he supposed. But it was hardly the meal he'd imagined. She'd spent the whole damn time talking to Milos. And his cousin had spent the whole damn evening flirting with her. Yiannis had spent his meal cutting and chewing his steak with far more ferocity than absolutely necessary.

Then Milos had invited her to go out with him. Yiannis had very nearly gone straight across the table and grabbed his cousin by the throat. He refused to examine the reason for that. She was engaged, of course. She shouldn't be going out with anybody, least of all his lady-killer cousin.

Now Yiannis shrugged his still tense shoulders against the wall behind him and tried to get into the moment. There were plenty of attractive, vibrant girls right here. One of them, over by the bar, had red hair just a shade darker than Cat's. And there were a couple who had the same long legs and tall, willowy frame. But the sight just reminded him of how she'd looked in the T-shirt and panties he'd seen her in last night. Remembered how his body had reacted—how it always reacted around Cat MacLean.

Irritably he shoved away from the wall. Milos was making no progress getting back with the beers. In fact, he'd stopped trying and had offered one of the beers to the blonde girl and stood with one arm braced against a pillar as he leaned close to hear what she was saying.

A soft hand brushed down Yiannis's forearm, and he looked around to see a brunette smiling at him. She batted her lashes. "Hi. I'm Marnie. Are you just visiting?"

"Seems like," Yiannis said.

"Me, too." She moved closer, and her breasts brushed against him. "Let's get out of here." Luminous blue eyes looked beseechingly up into his.

They left him cold. Every one of these women was going to leave him cold. He knew it. He glanced at his watch. "Thanks, but I've got to run." And without a backward glance—he had no doubt Milos could take care of himself—he turned and went out the door.

He walked back to the house the long way, making a detour to walk along the sidewalk by the shore. It was quiet away from the main business street. He could hear the waves lapping against the sand, and in the distance caught the ring of a buoy. Somewhere overhead he heard the engines of one of the last evening flights taking off from John Wayne.

He'd walked this pavement with plenty of women. But in the silence memories of only one walked with him tonight. The memories made him edgy and out of sorts. It wasn't just those of Cat in bed with him or on the beach with him or snuggled up against him on the sofa as they read the papers on a lazy Sunday morning. It was the Cat he'd seen this afternoon—the one who fretted over her grandmother, the one who held Harry as if he were a bomb she wasn't quite sure how to defuse, but she wasn't going to admit she couldn't.

He walked all the way around the island. Twice. Then he went home and worked on the old lawyer's glass-fronted bookcase he was taking apart and refinishing. He tried to lose himself in it—or let it free him to think about whatever his mind wanted to explore.

But his mind only wanted to explore one thing tonight.

He gave up and went to bed.

He lay on his back and closed his eyes so he wouldn't look at the windows of the apartment above the garage. He tried not to think about the woman who was there.

He didn't want what she wanted. But apparently he didn't

want what Milos wanted, either—or not with any woman other than Cat.

He couldn't sleep. Midnight turned to one. One became two. And he was still awake when there was a rapping sound on the back door. Tino's would have just closed, and Milos, damn it, must have forgotten his key.

So he hadn't got lucky then? That was surprising. He looked to have been making all the right moves.

It would serve him right if Yiannis left him to sleep on the chaise longue all night. Except Milos being the intrepid flirt that he was, he might climb the stairs and wake up Cat, grinning and asking to spend the night there.

Yiannis threw back the sheet and the thin blanket and padded to the back door, flicked on the light and jerked the door open.

"I'm sorry to bother you," said Cat.

CHAPTER FIVE

"WHAT'S wrong?" Yiannis demanded. "Where's Harry?"

Cat, her arms wrapped across her breasts, just shook her head. Her eyes were huge and her hair was flying all over the place. Her freckles threatened to take over the entire western world. "He won't stop crying."

She looked like she was about to start crying herself.

But the fact that this was only about the crying made Yiannis take a breath of relief. "He will." But even as he reassured her, Yiannis knew her desperation personally. He'd felt it himself last night.

"I've tried everything. I've given him bottles. I've fed him food. I've carried him and rocked him and patted him on the back. He just keeps screaming."

"Ever since you left?" Yiannis stared at her.

"Not quite. When I went to put him down. Stop looking at me like that. I didn't do anything!"

She didn't have to. She just had to stand there and he couldn't help staring. His reaction had little to do with Harry and everything to do with the woman on his doorstep. She wasn't wearing merely a T-shirt and panties this time. She was fully dressed in shorts and a long-sleeve pullover, but he had to ball his fingers into fists to keep from reaching for her. Maybe it was her vulnerability, the desperation on her face. Maybe it was that seeing her again over the past twenty-four hours had made him realize how much he'd missed her. Maybe it was that he remembered all too well the way she felt in his arms.

But he had no pockets to stuff his hands in. And in fact he was in serious danger of making his interest quite clear.

Figuring the knock at the door was Milos, Yiannis had answered it wearing only his boxers, and they were going to betray him if he didn't get some shorts on quick.

"Go back up. I'll be there in a minute."

She didn't argue. She just gave him a grateful smile. "Th-thank you." And then she turned and hurried back toward the stairs to the apartment.

Yiannis strode back into his room and yanked on a pair of jeans and a sweatshirt. It was March. The nights were cool—and jeans were less likely to betray him than a pair of shorts. Or maybe he'd get a grip and remember that this was Cat who wanted love and family and forever. That surely ought to dampen his ardor.

He could hear Harry crying before he was halfway across the patio. It was the same distraught sound he'd heard the night before. He knew first-hand how it could make you doubt your wisdom, your intelligence, and your ability to deal with a small person's needs.

He pounded up the steps and pushed open the door which Cat had left ajar. She was pacing away from him, making a circuit of the living room with Harry sobbing uncontrollably in her arms. For a small boy he had a powerful set of lungs. Yiannis could see his face screwed up, eyes closed, over Cat's shoulder. Then he opened them, and stopped mid-cry at the sight of Yiannis in the doorway.

The sudden silence and a single hiccupped sob had her spinning around.

"Oh, fine," she said in a tone somewhere between asperity and relief. "One look at you and he quits."

But just as Yiannis was about to grin and do his "aw shucks" routine, Harry's face crumpled and he began to bellow again.

"When did this start?"

Cat shook her head. "First I gave him a bath and read him a couple of stories. Well, you know—" she shrugged "—he tried to eat the books more than listen to them. But we read. And then I gave him a bottle and he fell asleep and I thought everything was fine. Everything *was* fine," she insisted. "And then, about an hour later, he woke up. Fussing at first. Then crying. Then screaming. Like this." She didn't need to explain.

"He cried last night, too."

"He wasn't crying when I woke you. He was asleep."

"On my chest."

She looked at his. "The chest was significant?"

Yiannis shrugged. "It worked."

"So you think, if I lie down with him on my chest..." Cat ventured.

Sudden visions of Cat with a baby nestled against her breasts danced in his brain—and started to have an effect on the rest of him.

"I'll do it," Yiannis said abruptly and lifted the howling baby out of Cat's arms. "Shhh," he told Harry, rocking him. "It's all right."

Harry clearly disagreed. But the sudden transfer from Cat's arms to Yiannis's distracted him momentarily. He looked into Yiannis's face with something like surprise and then recognition. Then he grasped Yiannis's hand and began to gnaw on his fingers.

"Ow." Yiannis started to pull them away, but when Harry's small face puckered up to let go with another wail, he immediately put his fingers back, easing them to the side against Harry's gums and not his very sharp front teeth.

The baby glommed down hard on them.

"Teething," Yiannis decided. Harry had probably been teething last night, too. But he hadn't considered that then. Now he said to Cat, "Does Maggie have any brandy?"

"You want a drink? Now?"

"Not for me. For him." He dipped his head and his lips touched Harry's damp hair. The little boy wasn't crying now, but he was grinding his gums against Yiannis's fingers. He had very powerful jaws.

"You can't give him brandy!" Cat was staring at him as if he'd lost his mind.

"Not a glass full. My mother used to rub it on babies' gums. Numbed them."

Cat looked at him doubtfully. "Misty would probably have us arrested for child abuse."

"We could have Misty arrested for child neglect," Yiannis countered. "Who's here and who dumped him and went to Germany?"

"She left him with Gran."

"And Maggie left him with me. And you. So…does she have brandy or not?"

"Not. But now that you mention teething—" She went into the kitchen and began rummaging through the cabinets, then spun around, holding up a small dark brown bottle.

"What's that?"

"Gran's cure. Vanilla extract." She was unscrewing the cap as she spoke. "I hope this works."

Yiannis did, too. He figured it was much the same principle as his mother's brandy cure. And he was pretty sure this was teething, because when he pulled his fingers out of Harry's mouth, the little boy once more began to wail.

"Put a bit in a bowl," Yiannis instructed, and when she did, he dipped a finger in, then poked it in Harry's open mouth again and began to rub it on Harry's sore gums. Harry's eyes widened. He hiccupped a sob, then he glommed onto Yiannis's fingers, crushing them between his gums.

"Better?" Yiannis asked him.

Harry gave a loud sniffle. But even as he sniffled, Harry pressed closer to Yiannis's chest and laid his head against Yiannis's shoulder.

"I'll take him," Cat offered.

But Yiannis shook his head. He didn't want any more visions of Cat carrying a baby. "He's all right." Slowly he began to walk the length of the living room and back again with Harry's small body snug against him. Harry's mouth worked against his fingers. He didn't cry. The sobs had turned into occasional sniffles. Finally after he'd made several more circuits of the room, Cat said in barely more than a whisper, "His eyes are closing." She sounded as if she was afraid to believe it. "Maybe he's going to sleep."

"We can hope." But he kept walking just to make sure. And he wasn't ready to go home. Not now. Not yet.

"I think he's asleep," Cat said. "His head is sinking."

It was nestled against his shoulder. She was right. Harry was completely limp. Sound asleep.

"Well," Cat said. "Thank you."

Yiannis grunted. "It was your idea."

"I'm sure the brandy would have worked," she said. "But you know what doctors are saying these days. And if Misty found out—"

"Misty isn't here. So she's got nothing to complain about."

"She would, though," Cat said. "If I did it, she'd complain."

"No love lost?"

Cat shook her head. "She always…resented me. When I moved in with Gran and Walter, her nose was out of joint. Even though she had parents and mine had died, she was always sort of—I don't know—jealous, I guess. She wanted whatever I had. Like y—" Abruptly Cat closed her mouth and wrapped her arms across her breasts.

Yiannis raised his brows. "Like?" he queried.

But Cat shook her head. "Never mind. He's sound asleep now. Look at him."

Yiannis didn't. "Like me?" he pressed her.

Cat opened her mouth, then pressed her lips into a thin line. "For all the difference it would have made," she said finally.

"I was never interested in Misty." But he did remember Misty making a play for him.

Cat shrugged. "It doesn't matter. Does it?" There was challenge in her eyes.

Yiannis sighed. "I wasn't trying to hurt you."

"I know that," she said sharply. "You were just telling me the truth. I've got it. I accept it. I've moved on." She held up her hand and flashed her engagement ring at him, in case he didn't get what she was telling him.

He got it. His jaw tightened.

Cat spread her hands. "And you've done…whatever it is you do. So since Harry's finally asleep, can we just put him to bed?" She looked equal parts annoyed and exhausted, and once more Yiannis felt an overwhelming urge to take her in his arms.

But he already had someone in his arms. "Of course," he said now. "Lead on."

"Thank you." Cat opened the door so he could carry Harry in to lay him in the crib.

He did, then eased away and turned. Maggie's bed lay between them—rumpled and unmade because Cat had already been asleep in it.

Now she stared at him across the expanse of twisted sheets. They had twisted plenty of sheets. Now their gazes locked, and all his memories of Cat in bed came flooding back.

Cat wild in his arms. Cat trembling in the throes of passion. Cat's fingernails digging into his back, her tongue tangling with his, her body welcoming him in. But it wasn't only the love-making he remembered. There were other memories, too, ones of waking to find Cat snuggled close with her body pressed against his, their legs entwined, her cheek on his bare chest, his lips touching her hair.

He'd always loved her hair. It always seemed to have a mind of its own. It was springy and curly and always smelled of fresh air and cinnamon. And he had relished tangling his fingers in that hair. Sometimes he moved on, stroking her soft skin and awakening her with kisses.

Sometimes Cat had awakened him, nibbling her way across his chest and nipping at his jaw line. Sometimes using her lips wasn't enough. Her hands were never still. They had played havoc with his control, touching and caressing, making him moan.

He damn near moaned now.

Cat looked sharply away. "Congratulations," she said. "You've done it." Then she turned and walked briskly out of the room.

Yiannis stared after her. Done it? Hardly. He hadn't done nearly enough, as far as he was concerned.

But he wasn't going to do it, was he? She was engaged. Marrying another man. Mouth twisting, he gave those tangled sheets a fleeting touch as he followed her out. He expected she would offer him a glass of wine, a seat on the sofa, a chance to wind down and celebrate Harry's slumber. He would settle for that.

But she had gone straight to the front door and was holding it open for him. "Thank you, Yiannis," she said briskly. "Good night."

He couldn't quite hide his surprise. And she didn't hide her eagerness to have him gone. He could see the edginess in her still, but this had nothing to do with Harry's crying. It had, he suspected, everything to do with those few moments they'd spent looking into each other's eyes.

So she felt it, too. The attraction. The need. The desire. She wouldn't be so eager to get rid of him otherwise.

Even as he thought it, she opened the door wider as if doing so would get him out of it faster. Yiannis slowed his pace even more, crossing the room slowly, then stopping right in front of her so that mere inches separated them. He looked down at her, watched her lashes flutter. Noted the heightened contrast between her freckles and her skin the longer he looked. Studied the quickening rise and fall of her breasts beneath the cotton of her shirt.

"Good night, Yiannis," she said through her teeth this time. She wasn't looking up at him. Her gaze was aimed somewhere just past his left shoulder.

"Not yet," he said softly.

Her eyes flicked up nervously to collide with his. "What do you mean, not yet?"

"I think a reward is in order."

"Would you like a teaspoon of vanilla extract?"

He smiled. Then slowly, all the while watching her unblinkingly, he shook his head. "No. I want this."

And he bent his head and kissed her.

This afternoon when he'd kissed her it had been a spur of the moment thing, instantaneous and unpremeditated. A test. A taste. And over far too soon. But it had awakened memories he'd long since buried, had been tantalizing him all day and all evening.

He'd wanted more.

Now he took it. Took her. And took his time, savoring the taste as he moved his mouth over hers, coaxed her lips to part, to open for him.

He wondered if she'd press her lips together, refuse him

entrance, but she didn't. Her mouth was both honeyed and tart—enticing and compelling—making him want more. And more and more.

Her lips parted. In surprise? In welcome? Both? He heard her breath catch in her throat, a tiny thready gasp. He felt her lips tremble. Her whole body seemed about to do the same, but if it did, he couldn't tell.

She didn't move at all. Just stood stock still, not holding him away, but resolutely refusing to invite him in, either. She didn't press her lips to his, touch her tongue to his. She didn't put her arms around him even when he slid his around her. Instead she remained almost rigid in his embrace. And while he held her, he could feel the tension vibrating through her.

"Cat?"

Her eyes closed for a long moment. And then they opened again and her eyes looked directly into his, steady and unblinking. And she pulled out of his embrace and said in a cool dismissive tone, "I think that's reward enough."

"Cat—"

"Good night, Yiannis." Her jaw was set. But her freckles had exploded, flaming her cheeks. And he heard the tremor in her voice despite her coolness.

She wasn't unmoved. He felt the primitive satisfaction that came from knowing she wasn't as indifferent as she tried to pretend.

He smiled crookedly. "Sleep well, Cat."

"Yes, it's urgent," Cat said into the phone, doing something she never did—badgering Adam to put her before his work. "You offered to come this weekend, and I'm accepting."

Demanding, more like. She needed him here. She needed him now!

Adam sounded surprised. "I thought you had insisted you were capable of getting a dress on your own."

"I can. But I realized how important this night is to you. So I'd like your opinion." It was true, of course. But she didn't need Adam's opinion as much as she needed his presence. After last night and Yiannis's deliberate kiss, she needed Adam desperately—to keep her focused on what mattered in her life.

"I miss you," she told him. "A lot."

Or she wasn't missing him enough. Scary thought. But her judgement was obviously seriously cloudy if she'd stood still and let Yiannis kiss her that way last night. Those two quick pecks in at the hospital in the afternoon had unraveled her a bit. But they'd been nothing compared to the slow teasing temptation his kiss had offered last night.

She just thanked God she hadn't kissed him back. She hoped.

No! She was sure she hadn't. She hadn't completely lost her mind.

She never should have permitted that kiss in the first place. But she'd been still dazed by the look they'd shared across that unmade bed. The memories of times in bed with Yiannis had still been dancing through her mind, even as she'd tried to get him out of the apartment. And then he'd walked right up to her, so close that she could breathe in the scent of him, so near that she could count the stubbled whiskers on his jaw as she'd tried to look past him as she'd waited for him to leave.

But he hadn't left. He'd wanted his "reward."

And then his lips touched hers, did their worst, and even now her heart did annoying things when she allowed herself to remember it.

She forced the memory away and tried to focus on what Adam was saying.

"Loomis asked me to play golf on Saturday. It's important," he explained. "Not the golf, of course," he went on. "But being part of the group. I got in because of my dad—"

Adam's father was also a big-shot banker "—but that was the step in the door. My advancement prospects increase geometrically if I work my tail off and if I play ball with the guys. You know that."

"I know that," Cat said, trying to disguise her irritation.

But something in her tone must have got through to him, though, because he placated her immediately. "That's not to say I won't come, Cat. I miss you, too. I just can't come tomorrow after work."

"Then come down after your game," she suggested. "I bet Loomis has an early tee time."

"Yes, but then we have lunch."

"After lunch," Cat pressed. "Flights every hour into LAX."

"Fewer into John Wayne."

"True," Cat allowed. And then she went silent. She stared out the window of Gran's hospital room and didn't plead further. She'd already pestered him more than she should have, and she knew it. Adam didn't need a woman who pestered. She didn't want to be a woman who needed to.

But something was going to give if she had to stay here much longer without Adam's stalwart presence by her side—and she didn't intend for it to be her.

It had been bad enough before Yiannis's kiss.

All her old attraction had resurfaced the minute she'd laid eyes on him again. But she'd been able to keep it at bay. During dinner last night, Milos had provided a welcome distraction. And afterward, when Yiannis had gone off with him to Tino's, ostensibly intent on picking up a woman, Cat had felt both incensed and justified, telling herself he might be every bit as appealing as he ever was, but he hadn't changed a bit, either.

He was still the same playboy he'd always been, and no more discriminate than ever.

When Harry had awakened and started to cry, she'd certainly debated for ages going down and disturbing him. Only the little boy's frantic incessant crying had driven her to it. And even as she'd done so, she'd expected that, if Yiannis bothered to answer the door at all, he'd have had some bimbo lurking in the background cooing at him to come back to bed.

At least there had been no bimbos. Unless he'd left them in the bedroom, of course.

But since he'd come with her readily and had shown no inclination to hurry back, she suspected he'd come home alone. Not good. It made him even harder to resist.

Seeing him for the second night in a row looking sleep-rumpled and whisker-shadowed brought back too many memories, reminded her too much of the man she'd fallen in love with.

Foolishly fallen in love with, she'd reminded herself firmly. But it was hard to keep telling herself that in the face of Yiannis taking care of Harry. He was doing everything she'd ever hoped he'd do as a father. He was the man of her dreams—still—damn it.

Because he didn't love her. He simply wanted her. He'd have taken her back to bed last night if she'd been willing. She was sure of it.

And she'd be right back where she started—in love with a man who didn't want what she wanted, who was only interested in his own hopes and dreams, who didn't care at all about hers.

"All right," Adam said after the silence seemed to stretch for hours. "I'll book a flight for Saturday afternoon. Can you last that long?" He was joking.

"I'll try." Cat did her best to suffuse her own tone with a bit of humor, though God knew she wasn't laughing.

"It will be fun," Adam said. Now that he'd thought about it, he was warming to the idea. "We'll find you a dress. Go out to dinner. Somewhere romantic. A bit of candlelight and—"

"Don't forget. We'll have Harry."

"What? Oh, right. Harry." His tone shifted. He didn't sound enthused. "Yes, well, we'll think of something. Maybe that neighbor of your grandmother's can take him."

"Yiannis?"

"That's the one. He helped out before."

"Yes." But there wasn't a snowball's chance in hell of getting him to babysit so she could go out with Adam! She didn't even intend to ask him to watch Harry this morning. She'd called an old college friend who lived in Newport and asked for suggestions about babysitters. Claire, who had two preschoolers, had said, "Just drop him off here."

But she didn't think Claire would be wanting Harry on the weekend. Besides, she wanted to spend time with him herself. The more time she spent with Harry, the more she adored him.

And she wanted to spend time with him and Adam together—like a family. A taste of family.

A hint of the life she would have in the future.

Yiannis was planing boards on the patio, shirtless in the midday luke-warm March sunshine when Cat carried Harry down the stairs.

"Good morning," she said briskly, trying not to notice the play of muscles in his back as he worked on the wood. He had several pieces lined up, leaning against the wall of the garage. They looked old, as if they belonged to a piece he was restoring, not a new one. She was curious about them as she'd always liked learning about the furniture Yiannis worked on. But she didn't stop to talk. She'd seen enough of Yiannis.

He straightened and shoved his dark hair back off his forehead, then set down the plane and moved toward her, holding out his arms to Harry. "Off to the hospital?"

"Yes." She kept a grip on Harry who was holding his arms out to Yiannis as well. "We're just on our way."

Yiannis frowned. "What?"

"An old school friend has agreed to watch Harry," Cat said. She turned toward the door to the garage.

"What? No. Bad idea." Yiannis was breathing down her neck by the time she got to the door.

She turned and practically had to stand with her back against the door he was so close. "What do you mean, it's a bad idea? Claire has kids. She invited him."

"He doesn't know her."

"He didn't know me a day ago! Or you," she added, which seemed pointless as Harry was now wriggling in her arms and trying to launch himself into Yiannis's.

"And now he does," Yiannis said and scooped Harry out of her arms and into his effortlessly. "And he seems pretty settled. Did he cry again?"

"No. Well, once. Briefly. But I settled him down again," Cat said.

Harry was bouncing up and down in Yiannis's arms and patting Yiannis's cheeks with his chubby hands. Yiannis wrinkled his nose at the little boy and lightly nipped at his fingers. Harry crowed gleefully.

"Good. And he seems fine now," Yiannis said. "We don't want to upset the apple cart."

"We're not—"

"A kid needs stability," he said firmly. "Not another new person." There was something in his tone that told Cat she wasn't going to budge him on this. This was a Yiannis she hadn't realized existed, a protective Yiannis. A fatherly Yiannis. A man who put Harry's needs ahead of his own. It didn't fit with her memories of him, only her dreams—before he'd shattered them.

"What did you have in mind?" she asked warily. "You can't want to babysit again."

"I thought I'd go with you."

"What? To the hospital?"

"Yeah, and then we'll play it by ear."

"You're not ready to go."

"Five minutes," he said, heading to the house with Harry in his arms.

"I'll take him." Cat hurried after them. But Yiannis wasn't listening. He carried Harry straight into the house, through the kitchen, down the hall and into his bedroom. As if he didn't dare give Harry back to her. As if he were holding the boy hostage.

Cat had half a mind to leave Harry with him and take off.

But she stayed.

Foolishly, she stayed.

Because less than five minutes later, Yiannis reappeared in jeans and an open-necked pale blue button-down shirt, sleeves rolled to bare sinewy forearms. He had Harry on his shoulders. They looked nothing alike, apart from both having dark hair. And yet, the image was one of father and son.

It wasn't the looks as much as the easy interaction between them.

"All set," Yiannis said.

"Does Milos want to come?" Cat asked, knowing the short answer before she even asked, but hoping against hope.

"No," Yiannis said unsurprisingly. "Milos had a late night," he added with a grin. "And he could have a bit of a hangover when he gets up. What a shame."

Cat had to laugh at the sound of satisfaction in his voice.

He kept her laughing all the way to the hospital. He always had—except when he was being serious. Then he had always enchanted her. Not much had changed. She knew better than to fall under his spell. Just because he was every bit the funny, charming, gorgeous man he'd always been—plus being good with a baby—that didn't mean she could let down her guard.

But it also didn't mean she could totally resist him.

She couldn't. Short of just sitting there all the way to the hospital, she knew of no way to remain distant and indifferent when Yiannis Savas turned on the charm.

He was too easy to talk to. He always had been. She might have been able to resist if he had overtly flirted with her. He hadn't. He didn't have to.

He asked about her work and she told him about her library job, going from branch to branch telling stories to the kids, making puppets with them and teaching them how to make fabric sculptures of their own.

"We use old fabrics the kids bring in and they create these amazing characters out of bits of fabric from their own past." Her eyes lit up as she talked. She expected him to stop her, but he listened intently as he drove to the hospital, and he surprised her by saying, "Kind of like what I do."

"You?"

"You use scraps and bring things to life. I do that with wood."

When he said it, she knew what he meant. While the job that brought in most of Yiannis's money had to do with importing and exporting fine woods, his love was for the wood itself—creating things with it and, even more, she learned, taking old neglected damaged pieces and restoring them.

"Bringing it back to life," she agreed, when he told her about the piece he was working on now—a seventeenth century Dutch lowboy that he'd taken apart piece by piece and was now cleaning up.

"I'm trying to restore it to its original spirit," he said. The wind was ruffling his hair through the open window and Cat couldn't take her eyes off him as he drove.

She thought he used the word "spirit" intentionally and accurately. There was an intensity to the word when he said it that spoke of the same feeling she had when she was creating a puppet and began to see its personality emerge.

"Was that what you were working on when we came downstairs?" she asked.

He nodded. "It's my sister-in-law's. It's been in George's wife, Sophy's family for the last 350 years."

Cat could scarcely comprehend that. "And you've dared to take it apart?" Its age and value would have intimidated her.

"It's a privilege," Yiannis said. "Besides, it needs help. It was pretty fragile, ready to topple over. It would never survive as it was. They need it to be sturdy enough to withstand a bunch of hell-raising little kids."

"They have a bunch of hell-raising little kids?"

"Working on it," Yiannis agreed. "One daughter, Lily, so far. A boy on the way. I doubt if they're done yet." He shook his head despairingly.

"Good for them," Cat said firmly.

Yiannis shot her a wry look. "If you say so."

She had, of course. Three years ago, which had ended their relationship, and now—to make sure he knew that she hadn't changed her mind. She needed him to know it. Or maybe she needed to keep reminding herself.

Spending the day with Yiannis and Harry was an exercise in being careful in what you wished for—because she had it.

It wasn't Adam and Harry. It was worse. The family she'd dreamed of, hers—for just one day.

He'd done stupider things.

Riding his bike off the roof of the boathouse when he was ten and breaking both arms qualified. Walking through the poison ivy wearing only his bathing trunks to retrieve a football when he was seventeen also made the list. Asking the gorgeous Lucy Gaines to the prom and forgetting he'd agreed to take his tomboy buddy Raquel Vilas was pretty much at the top.

Or it had been until this afternoon when he'd maneuvered Cat and Harry into spending the day with him.

Not because he hated it. Because he enjoyed it too damn much.

It reminded him forcefully that there was a lot more to like about Catriona MacLean than simply how good things were when they went to bed. There was her enthusiasm for her work. He'd forgotten how she glowed when she talked about the stories she told "her kids"—as she called them—and what they did and what they said and what their favorite puppets were.

She'd just been starting to work out what she wanted to do when she'd lived in Southern California. She'd obviously found it in San Francisco even though she insisted she was only a "substitute" and was still making a place for herself. He couldn't imagine any boss turning his back on an employee with that much enthusiasm.

She seemed to like the city, too. When he asked, she told him about her apartment on the edge of Chinatown. It was tiny, she said, but centrally located. She could get anywhere from there. And apparently she had to because she never knew where she'd be posted next. But she seemed to enjoy traveling around. It was exciting, she said. He liked the sparkle in her eyes.

"Are you going to keep working after you get married?" His question surprised him as much as it did her. What did he care what she did?

But he wasn't surprised when she answered, "Until we have children. Then I'd like to stay home with them." She glanced back at the car seat where Harry was babbling. "I'm not having kids to let someone else raise them," she said and met his gaze defiantly.

Yiannis shrugged. "Never thought you would."

It was clear that she was as fervent about family today as she had been three years ago. And having seen her with Harry, he could easily imagine her now as a mother.

Disconcerting thought.

Disconcerting day. He didn't ordinarily play at families. In fact ordinarily he couldn't imagine anything worse.

But he went along with it, just smiling when the woman at the admissions desk said, "What a sweet little boy you've got. He takes after you, not your wife, doesn't he?"

Cat's freckles had bloomed and she'd shot him a worried glance. But Yiannis had only nodded.

"You could have told her she isn't ours—I mean, yours," Cat hissed at him when they'd moved on to the waiting room where he was going to stay with Harry while she went up to see her grandmother.

He shrugged. "It doesn't matter."

It didn't even faze him when Cat brought Maggie down in a wheelchair so she could see Harry, and she looked at the three of them together and said with a smile, "You look like such a nice little family."

"Gran!" Cat's face was flame red.

"I was only saying," Maggie protested. "Not making a prediction."

"Well, don't," Cat said shortly. Then later, on the way home, she said, "I'm sorry about that."

"About what?"

"What Gran said. About you and me and Harry. She gets fanciful ideas."

Yiannis flexed his shoulders against the back of the seat. "No problem."

"I didn't encourage it," Cat went on as if he thought she had. "I have Adam."

There was something in her tone that provoked him, that made him want to provoke her in return. "Oh, right, Adam. Your dream man. All about marriage and family, isn't he? Where did you say he was?"

Predictably Cat bristled. "In San Francisco. Working," she said through her teeth.

Yiannis gave her a bland smile. "Of course."

"You don't believe me? Do you think I made him up?" She glared at him.

Yiannis grinned and shook his head. "No. But I was thinking I'd like to meet him."

Maggie had said only good things about Cat's fiancé, but even so at times he'd sensed reservation in her tone when she'd discussed Cat's marriage plans. He'd dismissed it, telling himself that no man would be good enough for Cat as far as her grandmother was concerned. Cat had got what she wanted, he'd told himself. Good for her.

So he'd turned a deaf ear. It didn't matter to him. Now somehow it did.

"You can meet him this weekend."

He blinked in surprise.

"He's coming Saturday afternoon."

Yiannis felt his teeth come together. "Is he?"

Far from being glad to hear it, he felt unaccountably nettled. His fingers tightened on the steering wheel, and he drove the rest of the way home in silence.

Cat didn't speak, either. She seemed preoccupied with her own thoughts—probably about Adam, Yiannis thought, annoyed.

Harry was fast asleep when they got there. "Now what?" Cat said as she opened the back door to the car and saw that the little boy was slumbering blissfully. "What if I wake him?"

"I'll carry him."

"What if you wake him?"

"I won't." He wasn't as sure of that as he sounded, but he figured if he woke Harry, they'd spend more time together getting him back to sleep again. Worked for him. He was oddly reluctant to call an end to the day.

He waited until she stepped out of the way, breathing in the tantalizing scent of her shampoo as she eased past him. Then carefully he reached in, unbuckled Harry and gently eased the sleeping boy into his arms.

Harry made a *whuffling* sound, but he didn't wake. So Yiannis nudged the door shut as quietly as he could and carried Harry to his place.

"What are you doing?" Cat was halfway up the stairs to Maggie's apartment.

"Putting him down for the rest of his nap," Yiannis said over his shoulder.

"His crib is up here."

"I'm taking him to my place."

"You don't have to watch him."

"I know that," he said gruffly. "But he might wake up crying and you'd have to come and get me."

"I would not."

"You did," he pointed out.

"Now I have vanilla extract."

But he didn't listen to any more argument. He opened his kitchen door and carried Harry straight into his bedroom and laid the baby in the center of his bed.

Cat followed as far as the doorway. "Yiannis, this is ridiculous. I can take him home."

"You could, but you don't need to. He's out." He straightened and nodded down at the sleeping baby. "See?"

Cat muttered something under her breath.

He raised his gaze and gave her a bland look. "Did you say something?"

"Yes. I said, what am I supposed to do now?"

He shrugged. "Read a magazine? Think about what we should have for dinner? Come and talk to me while I work." He tossed this last out, expecting her to turn tail and run.

But she said, "Will you show me the lowboy?"

He saw a light in her eyes, an eagerness that he instinctively responded to. "Follow me."

It was so unfair.

The man. The charm. The devilish enticing grin. But not just the physical attributes and the personality. There was the ease with which he dealt with Harry, the reverence he felt for the wood with which he worked, the way he listened to her babble on about her own work. He even asked about the puppets, for heaven's sake!

She should have said no, thank you. She should have just gone up to Gran's apartment when they got home and if he'd insisted on taking Harry to his place, she should have let him work—alone!—while Harry slept.

Instead, like some imprinted duckling or worse some besotted groupie, she followed right after him into his workshop and fell once again under the spell of Yiannis Savas.

The lowboy was going to be gorgeous. Cat could see that from the bit of it that he was rehabilitating. The top surface wasn't original, he told her. It had been damaged over a century or so of misuse when the heads of the family, a series of late eighteenth and early nineteenth century New York doctors, had stuck the out-of-fashion Queen Anne style cabinet in their offices and stored medicines and other paraphernalia in it.

Someone had put a new top on in the late nineteenth century, he told her, but it didn't look out of place to her. "How can you tell?" she asked, and he showed her all the clues in the changes and repairs over the years that told him the low-boy's history.

"It's kind of like your fabric critters," he said. "Their story is in their patchwork. The lowboy's past is written in the changes and repairs that have been made over the years."

She stroked her hand over it, felt the smooth wood beneath her fingers. It felt warm to the touch, like skin almost. It reminded her of when she'd had the freedom to touch Yiannis's skin. The thought made her cheeks heat and quickly she drew her hand away.

"I should go. Let you get to work."

"Stay," he said. "Sit and talk to me. It's boring by myself."

She blinked, then stared. He'd never invited her to stay in his workshop before. He'd let her in, had showed her pieces he'd been working on three years ago. But he'd never asked her to sit down and talk to him.

And he didn't look at her beseechingly now. In fact, if she didn't trust her hearing, she'd wonder if he had said the words at all.

He had already perched on a stool by his work bench and was intently taking apart one of the small drawers. Cat watched, her interest caught equally by the man and what his clever fingers and tiny tools were doing.

Mesmerized, she sat. She watched. She told herself she'd leave soon. But she was still there when Milos came back from surfing. She was still there when Harry woke up and clapped his hands when she picked him up out of his crib. She carried him back to Yiannis's workshop, and she was still there when Milos said he was calling out for a pizza and what kind did they want?

"Sausage and mushroom," Yiannis replied, "and a small vegetarian with extra olives and artichoke hearts."

Cat, who had been watching Harry pull himself up on a table, looked up, startled to hear Yiannis ordering her favorite pizza.

He met her gaze, shrugged. "How can you forget a weird pizza like that?"

Adam could. Adam did, regularly. Or maybe he thought that by now she'd realized how much better pepperoni was because he liked it best.

Cat didn't say that. She didn't mind pepperoni. And Adam was a man for the long haul.

Not like Yiannis who was tempting in every way—except the one that mattered.

Today had been a one-off, never to be repeated.

But even knowing it, when she finally did take Harry back to the apartment later that evening and put him to bed for the night—having declined Yiannis's grinning offer to come and hold her hand while she did so—Cat couldn't help standing in the darkness of Gran's kitchen afterward and looking down at Yiannis's profile through his workshop window.

He was sitting on the stool where he'd been much of the afternoon. His dark hair fell over his forehead as he hunched over one of the lowboy's damaged legs and carefully, meticulously repaired it. She watched as his hands moved over the wood, remembered times when those hands had moved as slowly, as intently, on her.

But then, all of a sudden, he smacked the leg down on his work bench, flung himself off the stool and disappeared from view.

Startled, Cat stared at the empty stool, at the abandoned piece of the leg he'd left on the table, and wondered at his sudden frustration. That wasn't like Yiannis.

Then, before she could move away, the back door to his place opened and Yiannis came out. She stepped back from the window, so he wouldn't see her, even as she caught her breath.

But he didn't look up, he yanked a jacket on and said something over his shoulder. Seconds later Milos joined him, pulling a sweatshirt over his head. Milos grinned, then said something else and made what Cat could only describe as "curvy woman" shapes with his hands. Yiannis's brows rose. He grinned and nodded his head. They didn't turn and come back toward the garage. Instead they went around the house toward the sidewalk out front.

Obviously they were walking wherever they were going. And at this time of night—it was just past nine—Cat knew exactly what was open on the island—restaurants and bars.

They had already eaten pizza with her.

No. Nothing had changed.

Yiannis was on the prowl. Again.

CHAPTER SIX

THERE was no sign of Yiannis working outside when she came down with Harry the next morning on her way to the hospital. She was tempted to just keep right on going without talking to him at all.

But she didn't because she didn't want to be accused of "running away"—and she needed to prove to herself that she wasn't. So she knocked on his back door around nine-thirty. It was still overcast and had that chilly March morning feel to the air that made it seem much cooler than the thermometer actually said it was. She shivered a little in her thin jacket while she waited for him to answer.

And shivered some more when he still didn't come.

She knocked again.

"Da?" Harry said hopefully.

It wasn't "Dada." Harry didn't know anything about "Dadas"—he'd never met his own. Even so, it was a little disconcerting to hear it.

"He's not," she said, just in case Harry had some erroneous notion.

Yiannis jerked open the door, bare-chested, unshaven and surly-looking. His dark hair spiked, uncombed.

"Oh, dear. I'm sorry. I woke you." She wondered suddenly if she'd awakened him alone. Her face must have betrayed some of her consternation because his glower deepened, but he didn't speak.

"I shouldn't have come. I just wanted you to know I'm taking Harry to Claire's this morning." She said it firmly, and was not going to be talked out of it this time—which was good because Yiannis growled, "Do whatever you want."

What Cat wanted to do was kiss him. She had always loved the look of him when he'd just woken up, had always delighted in rubbing her cheek against his stubbled one and dancing her fingers through his hair. The desire to do so now was pretty over-powering, but fortunately not over-powering enough to make her forget her good sense.

What she wanted to do had nothing whatever to do with what she knew was in the best interests of self-preservation. "I will. Go back to bed," she said, though she couldn't quite get that out as easily as she wished because she strongly suspected he hadn't been alone.

There, she said to herself after she'd buckled Harry into his car seat and was pulling out of the garage. You did it.

She had will power! She had common sense! Maybe she hadn't done what she wanted to do, but she'd done what she needed to do. Maybe at last she was growing out of the need for musical comedy endings.

"She's doing very well," Dr Singh told Cat when she ran into him during her visit. He'd checked her grandmother over, then met with Cat in the waiting area. "She's very determined. Very eager to get back to her own home. Mrs Newell is a remarkable woman."

"She is," Cat agreed.

"She can probably begin out-patient therapy in another week. We can arrange nursing facility care for her since you say she has an upstairs apartment."

"Yes. Or I was thinking, perhaps I could take her back to

San Francisco with me? We'd still have to find a place that was accessible for her. Mine isn't. But my fiancé's place is. Or I can find some place near me." She didn't mention Yiannis's offer. It wasn't her first choice—at all.

"That is possible." Dr Singh nodded. "It would mean connecting her with new doctors and a new therapist. But we could do it. You should talk to your grandmother. Whatever makes her most comfortable. She will work harder at getting better if she is happy while she's doing it and sees a future."

Cat agreed. "I'll talk to her."

She rehearsed it all in her mind as she went back to talk to her grandmother.

"Good news," she reported cheerfully. "In a week you'll be able to get out of here."

"A week?" Gran looked appalled.

"They're very pleased with your progress. Dr Singh said I can start to make arrangements for you after you get out."

"I'm going home."

"That would be great," Cat agreed. "But you won't be able to do the steps just yet. I thought you could come and spend some time in San Francisco with me."

"You live upstairs, too."

"I can get you a place in a temporary nursing facility," Cat said, putting on her best happy face. "Operative word: temporary."

But even so, Gran's face fell.

"Or maybe," Cat added, "you could stay with Adam."

Gran pressed her lips together in a thin line. "I doubt Adam would think that's a good idea."

"Of course he would," Cat said with more confidence than she felt. Adam was stable and stalwart—a banker, for goodness' sake. Flexibility wasn't one of his greatest virtues. But he was reasonable. He'd come around.

She didn't mention Yiannis's offer just yet. It had been spur of the moment. But then, that was Yiannis. He did things like that. But the truth was, he didn't want his life upset any more than Adam did. And he obviously didn't like curtailments on his freedom.

Having Gran as a house guest would be a curtailment indeed.

"We'll think about it," Cat said.

"I'll practice going up steps," Gran decided.

"When the therapist agrees," Cat said.

But from the mulish look on Gran's face when Cat took her leave, she knew that Gran had already made up her mind.

Harry had adjusted perfectly well to Claire and her children. She had two—a boy just a year old called Andrew and a four-year-old girl called Izzy. Izzy loved babies, according to Claire, and it was obvious that she adored Harry. Harry pretty much adored her, too. Everywhere that Izzy went, Harry crawled after her.

"He needs a big sister," Claire said, laughing.

"Well, he isn't likely to get one of those," Cat replied. "But maybe he'll have a younger one someday."

She wondered if Misty had connected with Devin. Wondered if she had, how things were going. She hoped well, but she had no great hopes, which made her worry about Harry. What was in his future?

What would Adam think if she suggested Harry come live with them? Trying Gran out on him first seemed like a good idea.

"Thanks for watching him," she said to Claire.

"Any time. I wish you were closer. We don't see you now the way we used to when you were nearby. You could move back," she added hopefully.

"Not likely," Cat said. She didn't even bother to think about approaching Adam on that one. She knew his flexibility would never extend that far. He was a born and bred Northern Californian. Orange County was not in his future.

"Ah, well. Glad to see you this time." Claire gave her a hug. Then, as she was walking Cat to the door, she said, "Have you seen Yiannis?"

Cat wasn't expecting it, and his name hit her like a light punch. She shouldn't have been surprised. Claire had met Yiannis when they'd been together. She'd commiserated with Cat when she'd broken things off. Cat had told her why.

"There's no future," she'd said. "Yiannis doesn't want to be tied down."

"Selfish," Claire had summed it up then.

Now Cat nodded a bit warily. "He's my grandmother's landlord," she reminded Claire. "Why?"

"I ran into him a few months back at the butcher shop in Newport and I was surprised when he remembered me—and asked about you."

"Yiannis did?" That surprised her, too. That he'd asked—and that he'd bothered since he could have found out anything he wanted to know from her grandmother.

Claire nodded. "I thought he might have changed his mind."

"No," Cat said. "He hasn't done that."

He should have told her he'd take Harry.

But damn it, he wanted his life back. Ever since Maggie had broken her hip and Cat had come back into his life, nothing had been the same.

She'd been gone nearly three years. He'd been annoyed when she'd left, sure that she'd realize what a good thing they had and would come back. But when she didn't, he'd shrugged it off.

Yes, his life had been a little less bright without Cat in it. No one he knew could make him laugh the way she did. And no one else ever quite got in under his defenses the way Cat had. No woman had ever titillated his senses—before or the few he'd been with since—the way Cat had.

Not that he'd spent time thinking about it.

He hadn't. Then.

But now that she'd turned up again, the memories, damn them, had come back. They made him want her again with a passion that surprised him. They were the reason he'd convinced her not to take Harry to Claire yesterday.

They were the reason he'd spent the day with her.

Making more memories—which hadn't been the point at all.

He'd been hoping that somewhere along the line he'd decide that she was just like all the rest of the women he'd known: forgettable, replaceable.

It hadn't worked.

And having her there in his workshop last night had really screwed things up. He'd been glad to have her there—had enjoyed her presence, her comments, her conversation. But it had made him remember another time he'd been working on a project and she'd come into the workshop to ask him something, and she'd barely got a word out before he'd reached for her, kissed her.

She never had asked whatever it was she'd come for because she'd kissed him right back. And they'd ended up in his bed, hot and sweaty and sated—for the moment.

But with Cat, there had never been satiation. There had never been enough.

And that was exactly what had frustrated the hell out of him last night.

She'd taken Harry and gone back to the apartment—refusing Yiannis's offer to join her—and he'd been left edgy and frustrated.

He'd worked intently on the lowboy's split leg, trying to

lose himself in the wood. He could do that. He had done it often enough in the past. Wood was always his distraction, his focus.

But he couldn't do it last night. Memories of Cat kept crowding in, echoes of her laughter had haunted him. In his mind's eye he could still see the way she brushed her crazy hair away from her face, the way her freckles blended gold in the distance, the way she looked at him, her gaze warm and compelling.

It had compelled him right into leaving the lowboy's leg alone before he screwed it up, his fingers were fumbling so badly. It had compelled him right out the door, determinedly headed for DeSoto's, the bar he and Milos hadn't gone to the night before, the one where, he'd assured Milos, the girls were even prettier.

Not that he had noticed. He'd stayed until closing, drowning his distraction in beer—and in unrelenting memories of Cat.

The phone was ringing when Cat and Harry got back from Claire's.

Harry was gnawing his fist and kicking his feet and generally announcing how hungry he was. So Cat plunked him on a blanket on the floor and put a handful of Cheerios in a plastic bowl on the floor with him, knowing they would be all over the blanket before he got them in his mouth.

It didn't matter. She knew that now. She knew Harry now. She felt a surge of love for him and reached over to ruffle his hair even as she reached for the phone.

"Hello?"

There was a hollow echoey sort of sound and then a pause, followed by a young woman's suspicious voice demanding, "Who is this?"

"Misty?"

"Yes. Who's this?" the voice demanded again.

"It's Cat."

"Cat?" There was a pause, then no joy at all in the next demand. "What are *you* doing there?" There was a wealth of suspicion in the words.

"Trying to get hold of you," Cat said, irritated but refusing to bristle. "I've left messages."

"Why? What's happened? Oh my God. It's Harry!" There was, Cat was surprised to hear, a note of genuine panic in her voice.

"It's not Harry—"

But Misty cut her off. "My phone doesn't work over here. I knew something would happen! I've been calling and calling every time I could get to a pay phone. But no one's ever home! What's going on? Where's Gran? Why are you leaving me messages? Where's Harry?" Each question became more shrill than the last.

"Harry's right here. Eating Cheerios."

"Oh." The very prosaicness seemed to allow Misty to take a breath. And once more Cat was surprised—this time at the amount of relief she'd heard in that one word. "Well, good," Misty added. "But then where's Gran? Why are you there?" The suspicion was creeping back. "What's going on, Cat? Why have you got Harry?"

"I'm trying to tell you," Cat said with a bit less patience than was probably warranted. "Gran broke her hip. She's in the hospital."

"Oh, my God. What happened?"

As briefly as possible Cat outlined the sequence of events, ending with, "I tried to let you know as soon as I got here. I called and left messages. Lots of them."

"Well, I would have left messages, too," Misty said stoutly. "But Gran doesn't have a machine, you know. It's not like I just left and didn't bother."

And as much as that's exactly what it had seemed like, Cat realized that Misty was probably telling the truth.

No one had been home all day and all evening. By the time that she'd got home, Misty, halfway across the world, would have been in bed. Gran, of course, was of a generation that didn't believe in answering machines.

"I'm sure you did," Cat placated her. "I understand," she added soothingly.

"I don't think you do," Misty nearly snapped her head off. "He's my son! You don't have kids. How could you possibly understand?"

Cat felt as if she'd been slapped. Of course that's the way it had always been between her and Misty. A complete disconnect. It was amazing that Harry was such a sweet little boy. And it was for Harry that she said with determined calm, "I don't need to have kids of my own to value them, Misty."

"I guess," Misty mumbled.

"I've taken good care of him. Harry is fine."

"Well, thanks," Misty said grudgingly after a moment. Then, "Did he get his tooth?" She sounded eager and excited now. "He was teething when I left." Her voice softened as she spoke, and Cat heard something like real motherly concern in Misty's tone.

"He's certainly been teething," Cat agreed. She didn't mention the screaming. Or the vanilla extract.

"He cries and cries," Misty murmured. "Poor little thing. Sometimes I don't know what to do. I wanted to bring him, but…I should never have left him."

Cat was torn between saying, *No, you shouldn't have*, and not saying anything at all. Finally she said, "He's feeling all right now. And he loves the beach." She'd taken him down there a couple of times and Harry had delighted in the water—and wanted to eat all the sand. She didn't mention that, either.

"You put suntan lotion on him, I hope!" Misty yelped. "His skin is so fair, you have to—"

"I always put suntan lotion on him," Cat said.

Now it was Misty's turn to let the silence go on too long. Finally she said, "Of course you did. I'm just…worried. I'll be on the next plane home."

Cat felt as if all the air went out of her balloon. "You're coming home?"

Misty? Just like that? Drop everything for someone else? She couldn't believe it.

"You don't have to," she said. "I mean, Harry's in good hands. Really. Gran said you had…important things to do there."

She didn't want to spell out what Gran had told her. Misty had always kept her own counsel, and she certainly wouldn't have wanted Cat to know her business.

"You mean telling Devin he had a son," Misty said, jolting Cat completely.

"Well, yes, but—"

"It's what I came to do," Misty said matter-of-factly. "He called and asked me to come on his R&R. I was surprised. We'd broken up before I found out I was pregnant. And then him calling—it was a shock. I could hardly tell him about Harry on the phone. And I couldn't bring him. So I asked Gran to watch him and I came."

"It…must have…gone well?"

"It did," Misty agreed brightly. "We're married."

Just like that?

Cat couldn't form the words to ask. But she didn't have to.

Misty went right on. "When I told him about Harry he couldn't believe it. He was shocked. And then mad because I hadn't told him. But how could I when he was worried about getting involved with me. He broke it off because he was going off to the other side of the world and doing something he couldn't even talk about? Something dangerous, you know? He's in Special Forces."

Cat didn't know that, either. In fact, pretty much everything Misty was saying was a revelation to her.

"But he's back on base at the moment. He's got leave right now. He said he realized that he could die anywhere—and he didn't want his life to be without me. Isn't that beautiful?" Misty sounded close to tears.

"It is," Cat agreed, and couldn't help but feel a little envious.

"He's so eager to see Harry. And he has a week or so left at least. Wait'll I tell him. We'll be there quick as we can."

"Misty, I—"

"I'll call you. Give my boy kisses from his mama."

And just like that, Misty was gone.

It was so like her. Mercurial, spontaneous, determined to get her own way. And yet not like her, either. This Misty was apparently committed, reasonably responsible, surprisingly maternal. And *married.*

Cat stood there, stunned, still holding the receiver, until Harry let out a shriek, making it clear that Cheerios weren't going to be enough.

She intended to take Harry back to Claire's just for an hour or so Saturday morning, but the phone woke her at shortly past seven.

"Bring Harry here when you go to the hospital this morning," Yiannis said peremptorily.

"I can take him to Claire's," Cat said, struggling to wake up. Harry was just stirring now, awakened by the phone.

"Were you asleep?" Yiannis demanded suspiciously.

"No, er, well, yes. What difference does it make?"

He muttered something under his breath. "Sorry," he said. "I thought Harry would have you up by now."

"Harry kindly let me sleep in." Cat smiled over at the little boy who was now sitting up and regarding her solemnly. He lifted his arms so she could pick him up. "We have an understanding."

"Lucky you," Yiannis said drily. But it sounded as if he meant it.

And it was true. She felt lucky for having had these days with Harry. She and Harry were a team, as far as she was concerned. And she didn't like the thought of Misty coming back and taking him away. She sighed as Harry dragged himself to his feet. "Misty's coming home."

"What? When?" He sounded as surprised as she'd felt.

Harry let out a yell when she didn't immediately lift him out.

"Tomorrow," Cat said. "Gotta go."

"Bring him down," Yiannis commanded before she hung up.

"But—"

"Just do it. You can tell me about Misty."

Cat wasn't sure she shouldn't just take Harry to Claire's anyway. But if she didn't show up at Yiannis's, he would no doubt accuse her of "running away." So when she had Harry fed and dressed and she'd showered and eaten breakfast, she carried him downstairs.

Yiannis opened the door to the back patio just as she did, so there was no chance to change her mind. His hair was tousled and his jaw still stubbled, but he was dressed, at least, though his feet were bare.

He took Harry out of her arms. "I thought Maggie said two weeks."

Cat shrugged helplessly. "Yes, well, apparently she has a maternal bone in her body. Or she's not quite sure she trusts me to take care of him."

"She said that?" Yiannis was clearly offended.

Cat shrugged. "She implied it. But I'm not surprised. She's often just snarky about me. But this time I think she was genuinely concerned about Harry."

"Which is why she never called."

"Apparently she did. But we were never there. And that's true. Now that she knows, she intends to cut things short and come home at once. Of course," she added drily, "her mission was accomplished."

"Mission?"

"She got married."

Yiannis looked as astonished as she'd been. "To the Marine?"

"He's Army," Cat said. "Special Forces. But if she told me anything else, she'd have to kill me. Or Devin would." She laughed, remembering Misty's rather flamboyant comments about Devin's work. But at the same time she still felt a sense of envy—something she'd never felt toward Misty before—because Misty had married the man she loved.

I am, too, Cat reminded herself sharply. *I'm marrying Adam.*

"They're both coming. Devin, too—to meet Harry."

Yiannis shook his head, still looking at bit stunned. But then a grin flickered across his face. "How 'bout that, Harry?" He reached out and took the baby out of Cat's arms. "You're going to get to meet your dad."

Harry grinned back and clapped his hands, then patted Yiannis's cheeks. "Da," he said. "Da!"

Cat was astonished to find that Yiannis could blush.

"Not me," he said, as if Harry had the faintest idea what he was saying.

But Harry was on a roll. "Da," he said again, slapping his hands against Yiannis's cheeks. "Da da da!" For the first time since she'd known him, Yiannis looked seriously unnerved.

"I don't think he's insisting on your paternity," Cat said kindly. "I think he's just practicing elocution."

Yiannis eyed her doubtfully, then shrugged. "Just don't want him getting any ideas."

"No."

Or me, either, Cat thought. But seeing Yiannis with a baby in his arms made it difficult.

Think of Adam, Cat told herself. *Think of Adam.*

And heaven help her, she tried.

But it was a great relief when at last it was Saturday afternoon and Adam showed up.

"Catriona." A smile lit Adam's face when he spotted her at the baggage claim.

"At last," Cat breathed and practically flung herself at him, accepting his kiss and kissing him back, fiercely, determinedly.

It was Adam who broke the kiss and stepped back, his brows lifting in surprise. "Wow. Maybe you should go away more often." He grinned.

"No." Cat shook her head fiercely. She shouldn't go away from him at all. Ever. "Did you check any luggage?"

He hadn't. "I'm only here one night."

That was true, of course. But a part of her had hoped he'd decide that he could spare a day or two and would stay longer.

"I head back early tomorrow afternoon."

Cat masked her disappointment as she looped her arm through his. "No matter. We'll have a wonderful time while you're here."

Adam slanted a grin at her as they walked to where she'd parked the car. "Where's this baby you've been telling me about?" He looked around now, as if he might have missed Harry lurking about somewhere.

"Gran's neighbor is taking care of him," Cat said.

It hadn't been her idea. She'd have taken Harry to meet Adam, but after she came back from the hospital and would have picked him up, Milos had met her at the door. "Yiannis took him to the beach."

"Now? Harry needs a nap."

"Which he can get while you're at the airport. They won't be gone long. He thought you'd be pleased," Milos had added. "Give you time with your man and all." He waggled his eyebrows suggestively.

"Yiannis said that?" Somehow she doubted it.

"Well, actually he said he'd teach him how to pick up girls."

That Cat had believed. "He already knows," she said. Harry could have had his pick of a dozen or more who'd stopped to coo and goo over him the last time Cat had taken him to the sand.

"We'll be back and pick him up as soon as we can." She waved her fingers as she headed for the garage.

Actually, for whatever reason he'd done it, Yiannis had given her a real opportunity to concentrate on her fiancé without distractions. And until Adam was settled into his visit, that seemed like a very smart idea.

So she did exactly that. As he slid into the passenger seat next to her, she turned and simply feasted her eyes on him, tried to memorize him, to remind herself of all the things she loved about Adam, all the ways he compared favorably to Yiannis.

It wasn't hard.

Adam was taller than Yiannis, a good six feet two to Yiannis's barely six feet. He was more classically handsome. Adam's hair was that wonderful dark honey tipped in gold that came from playing tennis and golf in the sunshine. It was meticulously cut and, even wind-blown, it always looked perfect. Yiannis's was that thick dark brown that was almost, but not quite black. It also had a lamentable tendency to curl just enough to never look quite combed. Adam's nose was blade straight. Yiannis's, she knew, had been broken at least once. Adam's jaw was smooth, freshly shaved this morning—or maybe right before he'd got on the plane. Bankers didn't do stubble, Adam had once told her.

His eyes were azure blue and his teeth were pearly white. He had perfect teeth with no tiny chip where he'd collided with his surfboard. He had no scars, either, not like Yiannis whose chin bore evidence of where his brother Demetrios's skateboard had clipped him.

Adam had no blemishes at all that Cat could see. He was pretty much perfect.

It wasn't only his looks that recommended him, either. He was bright, well-read. A complete gentleman with no rough edges.

Adam didn't tease. He didn't bait. He didn't argue. Well, not much. Only about her needing a new dress for the ball.

"The high end department stores," he said now as she got out of the airport and headed west. "Does Southern California have any?"

That was his one flaw—he had the Northern Californian's disdain for the southern part of the state.

"Surprisingly, we do," Cat said shortly.

He looked doubtful.

So she took him to Neiman Marcus. You couldn't get much more high end than that. Not even in San Francisco.

Adam sighed with relief when they went through the doors. "Yes," he said. "We can find something here."

Cat found something in about two minutes. Adam wanted her to try on several, make comparisons, evaluate the pros and cons. But Cat didn't need to parade around in dresses that enveloped her in ruffles or that made her look like a cupcake.

The dress she found could have been described as a knock-off of the sensational bridesmaid's dress at a recent British royal wedding—only in a deep dark blue. Cat tried it on. It fit, outlining her curves enough to allow her to prove she had some, dipping at the neck to hint at cleavage, and above all, not clashing with her dark red hair.

Why look further?

"You might see something you like better," Adam suggested.

Never.

"I won't," Cat assured him. And she was firm enough in her refusal that Adam gave up, glanced at his watch and said with surprise, "That took less than an hour. You must be the only woman in the world who could do that."

Cat doubted it. But she wasn't going to argue. She started to leave, but the saleslady, knowing a good mark when she saw one, said to Adam, "Does the lady perhaps need a shawl? The nights can be cool."

"And even cooler by the bay," Adam said.

So Cat chose a shawl.

"It's grey," Adam said, disgruntled. "Like a battleship."

It was a light silver airy shawl with a metallic thread interwoven so that it glittered subtly in the light. Against the deep dark blue of her dress, it looked, to Cat, like starlight, a gossamer milky way.

But Adam fingered a white one. "What about this?"

As a garment it was lovely. But not with the blue dress and her red hair.

"I'd look like a flag." She took off the silver one and handed it to the saleslady.

Adam wanted her to get shoes, too. But Cat said no. "I have shoes. I want shoes I'm comfortable in."

"Not those old sandals," Adam protested.

"No, not them," Cat assured him. She knew which ones he meant. She wore them to work. They were the most comfortable shoes she owned. "I have another pair that are more elegant." She used the word she knew would settle his fears. "We'd better hurry. I want to take you by the hospital before we have to go pick up Harry."

Taking Adam to the hospital was a bit of a risk. She wasn't sure what Gran would do or say. But she'd have a better idea of whether or not to broach the subject of her moving to San Francisco, specifically her moving into Adam's place for a couple of weeks, once she saw them together.

She held her breath when they walked in. But Adam was always polite and charming. And apparently Gran was on her best behavior. She was much more cheerful than she had been when Cat had talked to her yesterday. She must have realized that coming to San Francisco was a good idea and so was getting along with Adam.

She said all the right things about how nice it was for him to take the time and come down when she knew he was busy. And he said all the right things about wanting to be sure everything was okay.

He looped his arm around Cat's shoulder and said, "And how could I resist her telling me she needed me?"

Gran's brows lifted as she looked from Adam to Cat. "She said that?"

Adam nodded, smiling, and gave Cat's shoulders a squeeze.

Gran's gaze narrowed on her, making Cat edgy.

"I missed him," she said defensively.

"Of course," Gran said, but she didn't sound entirely convinced—not to Cat anyway. Adam seemed to think she was agreeing completely. "I'd have thought you were far too busy," Gran added.

Cat didn't answer that. She changed the subject, opening the dress bag and showing it to her grandmother, telling her all about the ball.

Gran admired the dress. But then she said, "It's next weekend?" as if she didn't like the idea.

"Saturday," Cat said.

"You'll be gone?" A light went out of Gran's eyes. "What if I need you?"

Cat's eyes widened in surprise, then narrowed in suspicion. But Gran just looked back guilelessly, brows arched as if in hope.

"I won't be gone forever," Cat assured her. "And you can come up as soon as you're released." She still wasn't sure whether to suggest Gran stay with Adam for those few weeks. So she said, "Adam can help me find a place for you." If he suggested it, she'd know which to do.

But Gran said promptly, "Oh, no. That's not necessary. I'm staying with Yiannis."

"What?" Cat stared.

"We talked about it yesterday. He said he'd mentioned it to you." She gave Cat an accusing look.

Rattled, Cat said, "Mentioned it—in passing—when you were having surgery. We hadn't talked about it since. I didn't know if he still thought it was a possibility."

"Well, he does. He said so."

"I don't know," Cat began.

But Gran was looking stubborn, and Adam said, "That's very nice of him. And much less stressful for your grandmother than coming up to the city. I can't think that would be easy on her at all."

With both Adam and Gran lined up against her—and Yiannis on their side in absentia—Cat knew better than to argue.

"We'll see," she mumbled.

"He's a dear boy," Gran said, satisfied.

Yiannis? A dear boy? Cat didn't think so. And why hadn't he told her he'd talked to Gran?

"He came to see me last night," Gran said. "Brought me flowers," she told Adam proudly, nodding at the bouquet of daisies on the table by the window.

Cat had seen the bouquet by the window. Now she looked more closely. "Those are your flowers!"

They were in a jam jar. And she recognized them very well. They grew in the patio garden next to the house.

"Yiannis's flowers now," Gran corrected. "It's his house. Besides, even though I planted them, he thought to bring them. It's the thought that counts."

Cat wasn't going to get the last word and she knew it. So she came over to the bed and kissed Gran's cheek. "I'll see you tomorrow," she promised.

Gran touched her cheek and looked into her eyes a long moment. And if she frowned as her gaze flicked for a brief instant to where Adam was studiously staring out the window, Cat didn't want to know. She straightened back up and gave her grandmother a bright smile, waggled her fingers in a tiny wave, then grabbed Adam's hand firmly.

"Let's go get Harry."

Adam Landry—that was his name—didn't look like a banker.

He looked like the Greek gods Yiannis had had to draw in high school art class. He was tall and broad-shouldered and had a tennis player's tan and a hundred dollar haircut. He shook hands firmly and smiled with perfect teeth.

Yiannis disliked him on sight.

"Any relation to Tom?" Yiannis asked the man whose other hand Cat was clutching like it was a life line.

"Tom?" Adam looked baffled.

"Guess not." Yiannis wasn't surprised Cat's fiancé was no relation to one of the best football coaches in America ever.

"He's an Atherton Landry," Cat said, as if that explained everything. In fact, he guessed it did—if you knew that

Atherton was a beautiful, exclusive small Northern California town—and one of the wealthiest communities in the whole country.

He was surprised that mattered to Cat. She had never been one to adulate wealth. Though maybe if it came wrapped in such a handsome package, she did.

He felt like gritting his teeth. Instead he gave them a lazy, knowing smile. "I should have guessed."

While he deliberately kept his tone even, Cat was no fool. Her smile disappeared. She shot him a hard glare. "I've taken him to see Gran," she said briskly, "and now we've come for Harry."

"Harry's sleeping."

Yiannis didn't know if Harry was sleeping or not. Milos had been keeping an eye on him since they got back from the beach. Ostensibly he'd been going to do some work. In fact he had spent the last hour and a half returning phone calls and writing up orders, all the while trying not to think about anything else.

Now what he'd been trying not to think about was standing right in front of him, and he wasn't just going to let her waltz in and take Harry off with Adam Landry "of the Atherton Landrys" without learning a little more about him.

"Come on in and have a beer," he invited.

"We can't—" Cat began.

But Adam's smile turned to a grateful grin. "Great. I could use one. And I'm glad to meet you," he said. "I've heard about you."

"Have you?" Yiannis's brows lifted.

"Not from me!" Cat protested.

"No," Adam said. "From your grandmother. Last time I was here," he explained to Cat who was looking furious. "She likes your flowers," he told Yiannis.

Yiannis grinned.

"Her flowers," Cat growled.

His grin widened and he shrugged. "Come on in," he said, opening the door wider. Then he turned and led the way into the kitchen where he opened the refrigerator and snagged out some beers. He handed one to Adam, then opened another and pressed it into her hands. "Relax."

She didn't, which he thought was interesting. The whole time she was there, Cat seemed to be walking on eggs. Or hot coals. She was jumpy at everything he said, and spent a lot of time explaining things to Adam, who didn't say much, just leaned against the cabinet, drank his beer and observed.

In fact the only people who seemed easy were Milos and Harry, who came in a few minutes later. Harry actually had been sleeping and was still rubbing his eyes sleepily when Milos carried him into the room.

"This is Harry," Cat said, taking him from Milos and turning to Adam, beaming. "Isn't he gorgeous?"

A little warily, Adam nodded.

Yiannis didn't blame him. Harry didn't look particularly happy. And instead of giving Adam one of his sunny smiles, he stuck out his lip and buried his face in Cat's neck.

Milos asked Adam about San Francisco, mentioned one of his sisters who lived there, and then they talked baseball for a bit.

"Give him here," Yiannis said, and took him out of Cat's arms, going to the cupboard and getting a cracker for Harry to chew.

Cat shot him a glare.

Yiannis shrugged. "Just trying to help."

"You're just Mr Helpful these days, aren't you?"

His eyes widened at her tone. "Am I?"

"Inviting Gran to stay with you?"

"That's a problem?"

She opened her mouth, then closed it again, and turned away. "Did you go surfing this afternoon, Milos?"

She could give an Inuit carver lessons in ice sculpture. Yiannis might as well not have been in the room for all the attention she paid him.

It was all right with Yiannis—for the moment, anyway. It gave him time to watch the way she dealt with Adam Landry—and the way the Atherton Landry dealt with her.

This Cat was not the one Yiannis knew. The Cat he knew had always been easy and up front with everyone. With Cat, what you saw was what you got. God knew she habitually snapped and hissed at him when he displeased her.

But she was deferential, polite and self-contained where Adam was concerned. Even about things that Yiannis knew she could not agree—like when the Atherton Landry made a couple of disparaging remarks about Southern California—she merely demurred, didn't put up a fight at all.

Yiannis didn't like it. Where the hell was her backbone?

But because his mother had raised him with manners, even if Cat sometimes didn't think so, Yiannis didn't ask. He just stared at her steely-eyed, wondering why she was bothering.

The most animation he saw from her was when she remembered that she had something for Harry.

"I bought it in the hospital gift shop," she said. "But I left it in the car. I'll be right back."

While she was gone, Yiannis turned to Landry. "You don't think Maggie ought to be in San Francisco with you and Cat?"

Landry shook his head. "Definitely not. She would hate it."

Yiannis had to give him points for seeing that. But then Landry went on. "And it's not good for Cat, either. She obsesses far too much about her grandmother."

"She's Cat's only living relative," Yiannis pointed out.

"Yes. And I appreciate that Cat owes her a great deal. But

she'd be fretting all the time if her grandmother was there. She needs space."

What she really needed, Yiannis thought, was someone to share the responsibility with. But Cat was coming back, so he tipped his beer to his lips and kept his peace.

"Here." Cat, triumphant, returned with a brightly wrapped yellow box.

Yiannis put Harry down on the kitchen floor so she could put the package in his lap. Then, together they opened the box to reveal a soft plush bunny. Instantly he grabbed it and chomped down on its nose.

"Harry's highest compliment," Yiannis said.

Cat took the bunny and tickled Harry's bare belly with it. "Bunny loves Harry," she told him. "Can you give him a kiss?"

He giggled and wrapped his arms around the bunny and gave it a kiss.

The glow of happiness on Cat's face was wondrous to behold. She looked almost teary-eyed. Yiannis could well imagine how she'd be with her own children.

"I know he has toys," she said, directing her words to Yiannis, as if he were about to point that out to her, "but he's leaving and I wanted him to have something from here...from me."

He didn't reply. He understood. It was Cat being maternal. It showed how far she'd come. She'd been a bit nervous of Harry at first, but she'd adapted quickly. She was a natural mother.

She'd be great with her own kids someday, he thought as he watched her ease one of the rabbit's ears out of Harry's mouth.

"I'm so glad you got to meet Harry," she said to Landry as she pressed a kiss to the top of Harry's head. There was a delight in her gaze when she looked down at Harry, then up at her fiancé.

Don't you want one? Yiannis could almost hear the unspoken words. And he thought of her with Adam's kids and something twisted inside his gut.

"Very nice," Adam said. But he didn't move to hunker down on the floor with Cat and play with Harry. He simply sat back and observed.

"I'm cooking," Milos announced. "Shrimp on the grill. Fresh pineapple. A little island pilaf. You're invited," he told Adam and Cat.

Yiannis stared at his cousin in surprise. First he'd heard that Milos could cook. Certainly the first time he'd offered. He shot Milos a narrow look.

But Milos didn't even glance his way. He was turning his brand of the Savas charm on Cat and her fiancé. "How about it? Then I'll babysit while you go out."

Now Yiannis really did stare.

"Sounds great," Adam said cheerfully.

"Er," Cat mumbled, looking dazed.

Milos took that for a yes. "Clear out then," he told them. "I'll call you when dinner's ready."

Cat and Adam took Harry for a walk.

Yiannis stayed behind, demanding, "What the hell are you doing?"

"Cooking." Milos flashed him a grin. "Or trying to. Hey, I'm leaving tomorrow. Just my way of saying thank you for the hospitality. Though maybe I should be thanking your mother, not you." The grin widened, then he nudged Yiannis's elbow to get past and into the refrigerator. "You're in the way."

"Do you know how?"

Milos shrugged. "We'll find out."

It didn't sound promising. But Milos said, "You think she'd say yes if you offered?"

Yiannis stared at him, confused.

"Do you think he's right for her?"

"How the hell would I know? I don't know him!"

"Exactly," Milos said. "And if you spend a little time with them, you might figure it out."

"It doesn't matter. I'm not marrying him."

"What about her?"

Yiannis stared. "What?"

Milos shrugged. "Just asking. Here." He turned from the refrigerator and thrust a package into Yiannis's hands. "Devein the shrimp."

The meal wasn't bad. Milos was a better cook than he'd given any indication of being. And what Milos said was true, he got to see a lot more of Cat interacting with the Atherton Landry.

And the more she smiled at him and simpered and said, "Yes, Adam. I agree, Adam. You're right, Adam," the more Yiannis wanted to spit.

He didn't say a word. He didn't have to. Adam talked enough for both of them. And Cat agreed with everything he said. Milos continued to do his impersonation of Mr Charm. And Harry threw food with abandon.

Yiannis just shoveled in his food and glared at all of them.

It was a relief when his phone rang halfway through the meal and it was his mother. Ordinarily in the middle of a dinner party he would let it go to the answering machine. Tonight he stood up saying, "I've got to take this."

As soon as he had, he wished he hadn't.

His mother was ranting about his father. Again. "He says he doesn't know if he can be here for the family reunion," she told Yiannis, outraged. "He's got some business meeting in Greece!"

"Mmm," Yiannis murmured. He'd gone out into the living room to take the call, but he could still see what was going on at the table. Adam was talking, Milos was laughing, and Cat was, at last, sitting quietly no longer looking adoringly at Adam, but watching while Harry jammed a cracker into his mouth.

Then her gaze shifted and she was looking at him.

Their eyes met. Locked. One second. Two. Five. More. He couldn't look away.

Neither did she. Then suddenly she recollected herself, yanked her gaze away, focused again on Adam Landry.

But the heat wasn't there. It was earnest, not intense. And Yiannis knew in his gut that while Landry was obviously a bright man, an educated man, clearly a handsome, wealthy, serious, intent man—probably, Yiannis forced himself to admit, a very good man—he wasn't the right man for Cat.

"Yiannis? Are you there? Yiannis!" His mother was speaking in his ear.

He gave his head a shake. "Right here."

"I'm going crazy. I don't know what I'm going to do about him!"

"It'll be okay," Yiannis said soothingly. "You'll manage. You'll think of something. You always do."

He hoped Cat would do some thinking, too.

If you were going to get married, you needed to be careful. You needed to be sure you were getting the right person.

He didn't want to see her marrying the wrong guy.

She wouldn't, he told himself as he jammed his hands into his pockets and glowered at her.

She was bright, intelligent, savvy. She would come to her senses before it was too late.

Wouldn't she?

CHAPTER SEVEN

IT WAS not a weekend to remember.

Not in a good way, at least.

Cat drove Adam off early on Sunday afternoon. She kissed him good-bye just outside the security gate, promising she'd be back in San Francisco at least by Friday, a day in advance of Saturday's charity ball. But it felt awkward.

The whole weekend had been awkward.

Instead of feeling closer after their time together, she felt even more distant. Estranged, almost.

She was worried about Gran, of course. She wasn't comfortable with Adam's easy acceptance of Yiannis taking her into his home when she was released from the hospital. It wasn't his place to do that. Cat didn't want to be beholden.

But she didn't know how to say that. Especially since Gran was delighted with the idea.

She didn't like the way Adam had been with Harry, either. He'd been polite. But you weren't simply "polite" to a baby. You doted on them. You smiled at them, made faces and talked to them. Adam had said about three words.

Of course Harry wasn't his child. She was sure he'd be devoted to his child. But a little warmth would have been nice. She couldn't help comparing his distance and stiffness with Yiannis's easy manner with the little boy.

And that hadn't made her any happier.

Having Adam here was supposed to make her forget Yiannis, not show him in a better light.

"—not listening to me," Adam said.

Cat gave a shake of her head and refocused on him as he smiled at her. "I'm sorry. I was…was not listening," she admitted, embarrassed. She shrugged helplessly. "I've got a lot on my mind."

"I can see that. I've been seeing it all weekend. Your grandmother. Harry. His mother." He paused and looked at her more closely. "Was I supposed to make it go away, Cat?"

She opened her mouth to deny it, but then had to tell the truth. "I'd hoped," she admitted.

His smile turned rueful and he shook his head. "Sorry. I tried. I told you what I think you should do with your grandmother. But I can't make you do it."

"No. It's her decision." She accepted that.

"You'll figure it out," he said with quiet confidence. "Next weekend you'll be back home. Things will look different."

"I hope," Cat said fervently.

"They will." He leaned in and kissed her again. She closed her eyes and tried to focus on the touch of their lips, tried to go from there to a future together, to happily ever after.

Adam broke the kiss before she did and glanced at his watch. "Call me," he said. And he went striding through the doors of the airport terminal. They closed behind him.

He was gone. And Cat was left with a pain in her stomach.

It only got worse.

Two hours later Misty and Devin appeared in the doorway of Gran's apartment.

"Where is he?" Misty cried, looking around eagerly. "Where's my baby?"

"Napping," Cat said. She was going to say, *Shhh, don't wake him.* But Misty shot past Cat and headed straight for the bedroom. Cat fully expected her to fling open the door and shout her son's name. But as she reached the door, Misty's movements slowed, and she eased the door open quietly.

Cat could only see her profile, but it was enough. She saw the tension in Misty's face melt, saw in it the maternal softness she felt herself whenever she looked at Harry sound asleep, saw Misty swallow convulsively.

Then she turned to the man who hadn't moved from just inside the front door. "Come here," she whispered, holding out a hand to him. "Come see your son."

Devin looked every bit the tough hard-bitten soldier that Cat had imagined. He was shorter than Yiannis, his face and neck deeply tanned, but the tan ended there. In a short sleeve T-shirt, his muscular arms were pale. His hair, buzzed short, was dark like Harry's. She could see Harry in his face and in the light blue eyes that flickered to meet hers as he paused on his way across the room. He nodded to her.

Cat nodded back, then stepped aside.

He stood over the crib motionless, just drinking in the sight of the little boy. Then his mouth worked. He drew a shaky breath and put a hand out to touch the boy's soft cheek.

"Isn't he beautiful?" Misty whispered.

"The most beautiful baby in the world." Devin's voice was ragged. Not remote. Not disinterested. A man who had just fallen in love with his child.

Cat felt obtrusive, like she was invading their privacy as a family. But when she started to move away, he turned. His eyes were damp. "You're Cat," he said.

Cat nodded. "And you're Devin."

"I'm grateful," he said, as if it were his name. "I will never be able to thank you enough for taking care of my son."

"I was glad to do it," Cat said. She shared a genuine smile with Devin.

And then to her amazement, Misty said, "I owe you, Cat."

There was a sincerity in her tone that Cat had never heard before. And her blue eyes were luminous, her cheeks were wet. And before Cat realized it, Misty flew across the room and threw her arms around her and squeezed her tight.

Cat, after a split second's astonished hesitation, hugged Misty back. Her own throat tightened, her eyes welled. She blinked hard.

But as they hugged, it didn't feel awkward. It didn't feel forced. It felt right. It was the first hug they'd ever shared.

Harry, Cat decided, had a lot to answer for.

"Harry's going to miss you," Misty told Cat the next morning.

Devin had packed all of Harry's gear and was carrying it down to Misty's car. Misty, holding Harry, had found Cat in the garden where she had gone because she didn't know where else to go. She had spent the night on the sofa reluctantly, having offered to go to a motel and give them some privacy.

But Misty and Devin had insisted that she stay. She had, but she'd felt like a third wheel. And when Harry woke in the middle of the night, she had been awake in an instant, and had had to stop herself going to him.

But it wasn't her place to do so.

As soon as she awoke again in the morning, she went out for a walk, not wanting to intrude again. Now she looked up from the weeds she had been pulling and got to her feet.

"I'm going to miss him, too," she said, her words heartfelt. "He's absolutely lovely." She couldn't help smiling as she said the words, even though she already felt an ache growing inside.

"You should come see him. You can," Misty added. "The valley's not that far. You're welcome any time."

Cat thanked her. "I'd like that."

They stared at each other and years of dissension and memories flickered between them. They both looked away. There was only so far you could go after years of estrangement, Cat thought.

But Misty had other ideas. "I'm sorry I was such a bitch to you," she said bluntly and made a face at the memory. "I was jealous. You had everything I wanted."

Cat couldn't help laughing just a little. "You mean like beautiful blonde hair and big blue eyes and guys falling all over me? I don't think so. That was you."

"You had Gran," Misty said. "She was yours, not mine."

"You had Walter."

"Grandpa liked the fish he caught better than me."

"He loved you. He loved both of us. He just…liked to go fishing." Barely a morning went by that Walter hadn't gone fishing. She'd never taken it personally. But then Gran had always been there.

"I know," Misty said. "But it's taken me a while. You always were smarter than me. But I don't care," she added when Cat would have protested. "I'm happy now. Happy with what I've got." And her eyes lit as she said the words. "I love Devin and he loves me. We'll make this work. And we've got the best little boy in the whole wide world." Her words were fervent and Cat could only agree.

"You do."

Misty gave her another fierce hug. "Thank you—for taking care of Harry. For holding the fort. For helping us be a family."

"My pleasure," Cat managed, past the lump in her throat.

"How did I ever get so lucky?" Misty marveled.

Cat didn't think there was an answer to that.

She was alone.

No Gran. No Adam. No Misty and Devin. No Harry.

No family.

Cat stared around the apartment and tried to relish the quiet. There had been moments in the past few days—especially during Harry's teething—when she knew she had prayed for a bit of it.

Not now.

Now it was hard to relish what not only felt empty, but lonely.

The cats were here, of course. She wasn't totally alone. It wasn't silent. Outside she could hear the occasional car on rain-slick streets. And if she paid very close attention, she could pick out the drops hitting the windows. The rain had started while she was driving home from the hospital that evening.

Fitting, she thought. It matched her mood.

She had spent the entire afternoon and early evening at the hospital with Gran after Misty, Devin and Harry left. She had even had dinner there, picking up a sandwich in the hospital cafeteria and taking it back to Gran's room to eat when her grandmother did.

"Why not?" she'd said with all the cheer she could muster. "I have no one to rush home to now."

Gran had been glad of the company.

If she could have figured out a reason to spend the night, Cat thought she might actually have done it. But by eight o'clock Gran was tiring and had begun to ask her if everything was all right.

"Of course it's all right," Cat had said. "I just felt as if I hadn't spent much time up here while I had Harry."

"Thank you," Gran said. "You did a wonderful thing for him—and Misty."

"I'm glad I was able to do it."

Gran smiled and reached out and took Cat's hand, giving it a squeeze. "You're a good girl. Now go home and enjoy your peace and quiet."

Cat wondered if Gran had any idea how very oppressive peace and quiet was.

It was a shock then to have it broken by a brisk rap on the door.

She opened it to find Yiannis standing there in jeans and a windbreaker, his dark hair plastered to his skull and glittering with rain drops in the glow of the porch light. And the very last person she needed to see tonight.

"What?"

But he didn't answer and he didn't wait for an invitation. He stepped past her into the room.

So much for alone.

"Yiannis. I don't feel like company."

He was dripping on the carpet, but not leaving. Cat sighed. She supposed she should tell him to take his jacket off.

"Did Milos leave?" she asked.

"Yes. He came to say good-bye, but you weren't here."

"Oh. I'm sorry. Give me his email address and I'll send him a note."

Yiannis grunted. He cracked his knuckles. There was some unreadable emotion in his eyes that she couldn't fathom. But finally he unzipped his jacket and reached inside. "Harry left this." And he thrust the plush bunny at her.

It was the last straw.

Her cup of loneliness overflowed. Cat reached for the little bunny and cradled its soft furry body in her arms. It was foolish, of course, to let it matter. Harry hadn't willfully left the rabbit behind. He'd liked it. He'd chewed it happily and given it a kiss. But it hadn't mattered one way or another to him. Cat knew that.

But it mattered to her.

Saturday afternoon when she and Adam had been leaving the hospital, she'd insisted they stop in the gift shop so she could get something for Harry to remember her by.

"He won't remember," Adam had said practically.

Of course he wouldn't. He was too young. But—

"Oh, God," Yiannis said now, appalled. "Don't cry."

"I'm *not* crying!" Cat snapped, even as the tears slid down her cheeks.

"It's a rabbit!" Yiannis protested. He reached out as if he would take it away from her, but she only clutched it tighter.

"I know what it is!"

"Cat." His voice was ragged. "It'll be okay. We'll mail him the rabbit."

"It isn't th-the rabbit. It's f-family." But she couldn't explain what she'd hoped—that if Harry had the bunny, maybe Misty would tell him his auntie Cat had given it to him. Maybe it would be a connection, a link. It would make her part of a family. "N-never mind," she sniffled and started to wipe her face against her arm.

But he stopped her, reaching for her, not the bunny. With a groan, Yiannis wrapped her in his arms and drew her against his chest.

"Yian—"

"Shh." And he bent his head and began to kiss away her tears.

A man could only take so much.

Desire he could combat. Need he could sublimate. Words he could battle.

But Yiannis couldn't watch her face crumple at the sight of a stuffed bunny. He was no proof against trembling lips. He couldn't fight tears.

Didn't want to, anyway.

Didn't want anything but what he had—Cat in his arms, her face pressed against his shirt, her gorgeous curls against his lips, the scent of her citrusy shampoo tickling his nose.

He drew in a long breath, savored it, then tipped her face up and kissed her cheeks, tasted the salt of her tears.

It wasn't why he'd come. Nor was the rabbit, in fact.

He'd come to make her see sense, to be her "friend," to tell her the truth—that she wasn't in love with Adam Landry.

And now?

Now—actions spoke louder than words. He'd make a hash of the words anyway. She'd argue with him.

She couldn't argue with this.

Cat didn't argue. She clung. She slid her arms beneath his sodden jacket and got closer still, closed her eyes and felt the touch of his lips on her face—her cheeks, her jaw, her mouth.

They'd been tender, gentle kisses for the space of a few seconds. But by the time he reached her mouth, they'd become more. Much more. The heat that had always flared between them could not be denied. The determined reserve she'd managed—or had tried to manage—since she'd arrived, now shattered.

Her lips parted. Her pulse pounded. The bunny slid away unnoticed to the floor as her hands tugged up his shirt and burrowed beneath. Hot skin over hard muscles quivered under her touch.

She made him quake. She always had. For three years Yiannis had told himself he'd forgotten how strong a hold she had on him. But the feel of her body against his, and all the memories came flooding back. The hunger grew.

Whatever he'd come for, now there was only this.

Only her.

He tried to shrug off his jacket, but its wetness thwarted him. It was as drenched as he was. She'd been right. He hadn't known enough to come in out of the rain. He'd been walking for what seemed like hours, trying to get his head together, to find the words to tell her she was making a mistake.

Now he knew he didn't need words. If he could just get the sodding jacket off.

"Let me," Cat murmured, and peeled it the rest of the way off his shoulders and down his arms, dropping it to the floor Then her hands came back, sliding beneath his shirt, cool and wet now against his burning skin. It felt good. It wasn't enough.

"Cat." His voice was ragged with need.

"This way." She nodded toward the bedroom. He kissed her all the way to the bed, hunger feeding hunger until he pushed her lightly back onto it. He wanted to fall onto it with her, rip their clothes off and bury himself in her. Their fingers fumbled. Her shirt tore. He cursed wet denim. But at last they were naked, flesh on flesh. Her skin was so smooth.

When he worked on furniture, he sanded for hours. Making the wood as smooth as Cat's skin, he'd once told himself. But he hadn't even come close. Now she lay on her side and he trailed his fingers over her hip and down her thigh, smoothing, savoring. Then he rolled her to her back and parted her knees and knelt between them, ran his hands up her legs slowly, tormenting himself as much as he tormented her.

Cat moved restlessly, watching him from beneath hooded lids. Her tongue touched her lips. At the apex of her thighs, his thumbs brushed against the softness of her, dipped, parted, teased. Her eyes darkened. She made a small urgent sound. He slid his hands back down again. Then up. Touched. Deeper this time. With a finger, stroked.

Her lips parted. Her hips lifted, as if she could draw him in.

She could. Dear God, she could. It was all he could do to resist for a minute. Prolong. Savor.

And then as he slid his hands back down her toward her knees again, she reached out a hand and touched him. One finger trailed lightly along his erection. Made him clench his jaw and tense every muscle in his body to keep from shattering right then and there.

"Cat." He caught her hand.

"So you can do it and I can't?" She turned her fingers in his hand and lightly scratched his palm. Hell, even that simple touch was erotic.

He shook his head, smiling. Yes, that was Cat. Contrary even in bed. He grinned and came down to her, parted her. Slid home.

For a moment neither of them moved. He held still, watching her, drinking her in as he felt her body tighten around his. The feel of it nearly undid him.

Cat looked up at him, her face mostly shadowed in the spill of light from the living room. But her lips were swollen, well-kissed, her cheeks flushed, her gaze intent.

"Well?" she said expectantly and gave a little wriggle beneath him.

Yiannis laughed. Laughter and sex—it was so Cat.

"Just thinking," he murmured. Not true. He wasn't thinking at all. He was enjoying. And he enjoyed even more as he began to move.

Cat moved with him, against him, caught his rhythm and made it her own. Their gazes locked, their hearts hammered. Cat's head tossed from side to side, her hips lifted, beseeching him. He moved more quickly, then gritted his teeth as he felt her body begin to spasm around him.

Her hands tightened against his buttocks. Her heels dug into the backs of his thighs. He gritted his teeth and thrust one more time, and then mind and body shattered as he spilled into her.

He came apart. She made him whole.

* * *

They loved once, twice, three times that night. Cat wasn't counting. She was in a world of sensation, emotion, desire. Logic had nothing to do with it. Only need.

If she woke in his arms and tried to be rational, she couldn't seem to manage it.

And really, why try?

She'd protected herself for three years, and look what it had got her. Three years older. Engaged to the wrong man. And now—right back where she started from.

And every time she got that far, his hand would cover her breast or slip between her thighs. He would stroke, he would tease, he would make her tremble.

He would turn her in his arms and make love to her again. And she would know mindless joy for moments.

Now Cat lay with Yiannis's body snug against her back, his arm curved over her waist, his deep even breaths stirring the hair by her ear as he slept.

Now what?

She couldn't help wondering. Wrapping her fingers around his hand, she pressed it against her heart—and dared to hope that she would still feel joy in the morning.

CHAPTER EIGHT

CAT woke slowly, languorously, feeling relaxed, sated. She started to stretch. Her muscles twinged. No matter. She couldn't move far anyway. There was a hard warm body against her back.

"Yiannis?"

She felt his lips curve against her ear. "You were expecting someone else?"

She rolled over to face him, her nose bumping his. He had a smile on his face, satisfied but not replete. She knew that because he loosened his fingers from her grasp and hauled her around and on top of him so that she lay face to face with him, body to body, and she felt his stirring beneath hers.

No, not replete. Hungry. Again.

He framed her face in his hands and kissed her. It was a long, deep kiss that promised another round of the passion they'd shared all night. And she didn't say no. She wanted it as much as he did. Wanted it now in the clear light of day.

They didn't speak, they just touched. And looked. She sat above him, straddled his legs and watched the way his fingers played over her skin, stroked her breasts, tweaked her nipples. Then he stroked down her abdomen and slid a hand between her thighs, cupped her, teased her, probed. And all the while she watched him, he did the same, never took his eyes from her face unless it was to watch his fingers find the center of her.

Cat caught her breath at his touch, then felt bereft when his hand left her, only to find herself raised and settled over him again so that she could take him in. As she did, his jaw tightened, his body tensed. The skin grew taut across his cheekbones. He held himself absolutely rigid.

And so did she, enjoying the moment, enjoying the feel of him within her. She looked down at him and smiled, then trailed her fingers down over his chest, circled his navel, bent to plant kisses on hard nubs of his nipples. Waited.

"Cat." His voice was a growl of need, of hunger. His fingers bit into her hips, to raise her and lower her again. But she sat back, wouldn't move.

"Cat!" His tone was urgent now. Desperate.

As desperate as she felt as the feeling inside her grew and grew. Then, "Yesssss." The word hissed between her teeth as she rose until he nearly slipped away. But before he could, she came down again, united them, drew him in.

Yiannis groaned. Moved. Surged up to meet her. Then the playing was over. There was no more waiting. No more teasing movements. Now there was only urgency.

Quicker. Faster. Frantic. Like a wave that carried them both up to the heights, then broke and tossed them over, plunging them down, and rippling away, leaving them spent, bodies slick, hearts pounding.

Cat, collapsed against his chest, could hear his thundering heart beneath her ear. Felt his hand come up to stroke her hair.

It had always been like this with Yiannis.

It was what she loved about being with him—that it wasn't just the frenzy, though certainly the frenzy and passion were there. But at the same time they could play and tease and tempt each other. They could talk and argue and laugh. Life with Yiannis was more than just going to bed with him. It was about all of him—of them.

It was love.

She knew then that she had never stopped loving him.

She raised her head from his chest to look at him. He was smiling. Something about him reminded her of a lazy, well-fed panther. It was the dark hair, the stubbled jaw, she supposed. She really should be thinking in terms of lions. He had that very masculine smug proprietary look of the king of the beasts, as if he'd staked his claim, as if she belonged to him.

It was the truth.

Then he said, "So much for Adam."

Cat stilled. "What?"

He shrugged his shoulders lazily. "I think we've effectively proved you don't want Adam."

She felt as if he'd punched her in the gut. Or worse, in the heart. Slowly, as if she might go up in flames if she moved quickly, she eased herself off him, wincing as she stood. She dragged a blanket off the bed and wrapped it around her so she wouldn't feel so exposed. "This is about Adam?"

"Of course it's not about Adam," he said, frowning. "It's about you."

"What about me?"

He heard the shrillness in her tone. "What are you getting upset about?" His brows drew down. He shoved himself up against the headboard of the bed and held out a hand to her, to bring her back to him.

But Cat just clutched the blanket more tightly around her. "Did you make love to me to prove to me that I don't want Adam?" She forced herself to spell it out. She didn't want any misconceptions.

"No! Well, yes, but that's not the only reason." He dropped his hand and started to scramble out of bed to come after her.

But Cat didn't need him proving anything else to her, thank you very much. She snatched her clothes off the floor, plunged into the bathroom and locked the door.

The door knob jiggled. "Cat! Cat! For God's sake! Open the door." It rattled again. "Cat!"

But Cat wasn't listening. She'd heard enough. She turned on the shower as hard as it would go, drowning him out. Then she dropped the blanket and stepped beneath the hot needle spray of the water. Then she turned her face into it.

She didn't want to know when the tears began.

She'd been a fool—again. She was in love with Yiannis Savas—still.

And he hadn't changed a bit.

He wanted her just as he had three years ago. And he'd been determined to get her, to make her his, even knowing she was engaged to another man.

And he'd succeeded, damn him.

He'd ruined her for Adam—probably for every damn man in the whole wide world. But he didn't want her for himself. Except for now—and maybe tomorrow. But not forever.

Yiannis didn't do forever.

He didn't do marriage. He didn't do family. He didn't do love.

Cat stayed in the shower until the hot water ran out. She stayed in the bathroom until her eyes no longer looked bloodshot. She didn't stay there until she was no longer angry. That might take years.

At least Yiannis wasn't rattling the door knob any more. He'd probably given up and gone back to his place. Why stay?

She opened the door to the bedroom, snagged her suitcase off the chair and began to toss her things in.

All at once Yiannis was in the doorway. "What are you doing?"

She didn't turn. "Packing."

"Why?" He came into the room, started to take her arm.

She jerked away, went to the closet, took out her things and rolled them up to stow them in the case. "Because I'm going home," she said evenly, still not looking his way.

"Don't be ridiculous. Your grandmother needs you here."

"My grandmother will be fine. She has a staff of doctors and nurses looking after her. I can supervise by phone. And maybe I will take her back up to San Francisco with me when she gets out."

"She'll hate it. You know that."

"Too bad. I live there. I work there. My life is there. Adam's there!" She did turn her head and look at him then. Glared at him, furious.

She wasn't the only one. Yiannis's dark eyes glinted. "You're not serious. There's no way you're going back to him after what you just did with me!"

"Well, I'm not planning on telling him," Cat said, goaded. "You're right about that."

"You can't marry him!"

"Don't tell me what I can and can't do!" She slammed the suitcase shut and dragged it out to the living room and started down the stairs.

Yiannis followed her. "You're over-reacting. I didn't just make love to you to prove some point."

"Fine. It was just a happy byproduct then," Cat said acidly. She flung the case in her car, banged the door and went back after the cats.

He got in front of her, blocked her way. "It's true," he insisted. "Though now I suppose you'll go and marry him for spite."

"Better than marrying you," Cat muttered, elbowing past him and pounding up the stairs. Not the truth, of course. She'd have married him in an instant if he'd wanted to marry her.

He didn't. That was patently obvious. There had been no "I love you" no "I can't live without you." Only "You'd be making a mistake to marry Adam Landry."

Bas and Hux were, fortunately, right where she could see them. So she scooped them up into her arms and dodging past Yiannis, headed down again.

Naturally heavy footsteps came after her. "Catriona! Damn it. Stop just a minute."

But she didn't stop until she had the cats in the car and the door shut. Then she turned and came right up against him. He was breathing hard.

"You don't listen! You never listen. Listen to this." And he grabbed her and kissed her hard, as if he were imprinting a brand on her.

She could have told him he already had. For life. For all the good it did her. Because when she listened there were no words, there were no promises. There was no forever.

She stood still under the onslaught. She felt her body quiver. But her resolve, this time, didn't waver. And when he finally pulled back, she said, "I'm listening. What are you saying?"

"I'm saying I stopped you from making the biggest mistake of your life."

Which was exactly what she'd thought he'd been saying. Just that.

Nothing more.

"Well, thank you very much," Cat said tightly and she twisted away, opened her car door and slid in. "I'll tell him you said so."

"You're not—"

"While we're dancing on Saturday." She said it to infuriate him, delighted to see the flare of anger in his eyes. Served him right.

"What about Maggie?" he demanded. "You're just going to leave her?"

"Hardly. I'll stop and see her on my way out of town. Good-bye, Yiannis."

"Cat!"

But she'd heard enough—or, in this case, far too little of what she needed to hear. She rolled up the window and put the car in gear.

But she couldn't think of a single good show tune to play in her head as she drove away.

Yiannis doubted there was a word in the English language to describe the maelstrom of emotions—all of them angry—he felt as Cat drove away.

He slammed into the house, banging the door behind him, and kicked the kitchen chair that stood in his way. His bare toes protested, but the pain in them didn't begin to dull the other emotions assailing him.

Nothing, as it happened, dulled those emotions.

Not sooner. Not later.

Not that day or the next.

Yiannis told himself she'd come to her senses, that she'd realize she ought to be grateful, not blame him for ruining something that was destined to fall apart anyway.

But no phone calls of undying gratitude interrupted his solitude. She didn't come back. She simply left him with a whole new pantheon of memories that were driving him insane.

She loved him. He was sure of it. He didn't imagine she could have made love to him that intensely, that sweetly, with that much abandon if she hadn't.

They had a lot to give each other if she could only see it.

But he sure as hell couldn't figure out how to open her

eyes. Talking to her wouldn't work. And it was pretty damn obvious that she'd had enough of his actions for the moment.

Which was just idiotic, because she'd been every bit as involved as he had. He hadn't seduced her. He hadn't done anything that she hadn't wanted him to do!

Every time the phone rang he hoped it would be her. But it never was. His mother rang another half dozen times. His sister called twice. He didn't answer them He didn't need to be bothered by family troubles now. He had trouble enough of his own.

The only people he talked to were clients and distributors—and Maggie.

He thought Maggie would be upset at Cat's leaving. But she took it in her stride.

"I've kept her long enough from her life," she told him when he asked about Cat the day after she'd left. "She has work to do. The children so look forward to her. And I think she needs them, too," she confided. "She's missing Harry."

He knew that. He got Misty's address from Maggie and told her he'd send the rabbit she'd given Harry on to him.

"Cat will like that. She loved Harry. I do hope she has children of her own one day," Maggie said wistfully.

Not Adam's, Yiannis thought. His jaw clenched. "Maybe she will." He remembered the maternal look in her eyes every time she'd held Harry. He imagined what she'd look like with a child of her own.

"—beautiful dress," Maggie was saying. "Did you see it?"

Yiannis jerked back to the present to find Maggie staring expectantly at him. "See what?"

"The dress she bought for the ball. It's simply beautiful. Like a midnight sky with stars." Maggie beamed. "She'll look like a million dollars in it."

Yiannis grunted. He hoped to God she wouldn't be wearing it.

"I told her to get someone to take a photo of her with Adam."

"I thought you didn't like Adam."

"He's a good man," Maggie said. "He isn't one I'd have chosen," she added. "But he might be right for her. Who am I to say?"

No help there, then. And saying, *He's not right for her*, would take the conversation in a direction he didn't want it going. Maggie would have questions, and he was sure she wouldn't like the answers she'd get from him. Obviously Cat had said nothing to her. He left it that way.

He mailed the rabbit to Harry that afternoon. He put a note in it to Misty, reminding her that Cat had wanted Harry to have it. He also sent her Cat's address which Maggie had given him. Maybe Misty would write to her, thank her.

It wasn't much, but it was the one action he could take that might not backfire on him.

After he sent off the package to Harry, he went home, picked up his surfboard and went out on the water. It was a raw damp March day and no one else was out on the breaker line.

But the waves were decent and the weather suited his mood. And the more energy he burned off, the more likely he was to sleep, which he hadn't done last night—or the night before.

Monday he'd been making love to Cat all night. The memories were more vivid than the waves he caught one after another until he was finally too tired to catch any more and dragged himself back to the house.

He ate a couple of pieces of cold pizza and then went out to his workshop. Last night he'd spent the night here, sanding the old lowboy he'd taken apart and was restoring for his sister. The work was supposed to soothe, but it hadn't. It was supposed to calm, but it hadn't done that, either.

Things weren't any better tonight. Half a dozen times he'd had enough and grabbed his phone to punch in Cat's number. Then half a dozen times he'd stuffed it back in his pocket again. She wouldn't listen to him. She would only listen to her heart. And that was, of course, best.

He just hoped her heart told her the truth before she married Adam Landry.

It was nearly eleven when he heard the doorbell ring.

It was so sudden and unexpected that he dropped the spindly leg he'd been working on. It fell and bounced on the concrete floor. He grabbed it, but barely spared it a glance when ordinarily he would have been checking it for minute cracks and damage. Now he simply tossed it on the old sofa he kept in the corner and strode to answer the front door.

He was covered with saw dust, sticky with flakes of old lacquer. He hadn't shaved. He didn't care.

There was only one person who would be ringing his doorbell at this time of night. She'd listened to her heart after all.

His own heart was singing the Hallelujah Chorus as he flung open the front door—and stared.

"Mom?"

He blinked, squeezed his eyes shut tight and opened them again. Malena Savas stood there in the flesh, grey hair curling in the damp, a black trench coat cinched around her. A suitcase on the porch beside her.

Suitcase?

"Mom?" he said again, wary now, frowning, worried. "What the hell are you doing? What are you doing *here*?"

She pasted on a bright determined smile. "I'm getting a divorce, dear. I've left your father."

CHAPTER NINE

"DON'T be ridiculous," Yiannis said even as he ushered her into the living room and carried her suitcase in. "You're not divorcing Dad."

His mother turned on him and slapped her hand on her hips. "Don't you start," she said. "Not you. You're the only one I can turn to."

"Me?" Yiannis stared at her, dumbfounded. "Why me?"

She undid the belt of her trench coat and slipped it off. "Because everyone else in the family would be urging me to go back to him."

"Mom—"

"Because they're all so 'happily married.'" She made the words sound like a curse. Then she turned and marched into the kitchen, just as if it were her own, and put the kettle on. "They don't understand."

Neither did he.

"But I knew you would because you don't believe in marriage at all."

It was his own marriage he didn't believe in, Yiannis wanted to tell her. He believed fervently in hers. He shook his head, wondering if he was hallucinating the whole thing. He hadn't had a lot of sleep. Maybe his brain had come unglued.

His parents had been married over forty years. They were

the bedrock of his existence. Of his siblings' existence. Of their grandchildren's existence. Hell, for all he knew they were the bedrock of the entire world.

"Where do you keep the cups?" she asked. She'd found the tea.

He got them out for her. "Mugs, Ma," he said, setting them on the counter. "I don't have tea cups."

"It doesn't matter. Nothing matters. Just ask your father," she said bitterly, dropping a tea bag in each of them.

"Mom, I think you're over-wrought."

She spun around, her cheeks flushed. "You're damn right I'm over-wrought. I've had it up to my eyeballs with that man. He doesn't want to face reality. He doesn't want to think he's mortal. Do you know what he said when I reminded him about the family reunion?"

"That he had to work." Yiannis knew his father.

"That he had to work!" His mother practically shouted his words back at him. "And not only that, but that he had to fly to Greece to do it. What is wrong with him?"

Yiannis just shook his head.

Her shoulders slumped. "I don't know, either. But I'm tired trying to fight with him. I'm tired of trying to make him see reason. I'm just…tired." She visibly drooped right before his eyes.

Swiftly he put his arm around her. "Mom, maybe you don't need tea. Maybe you need to go to bed."

"Maybe I do," she said wearily. Her voice was so quiet now that he almost couldn't hear her.

"I'll get the bed ready." He left his mother sitting in the kitchen with her tea while he made up Milos's room for her, then carried her suitcase in and laid it on the window seat. He wondered if he ought to call his father. Did his father know he'd been "left?" Did his workaholic father even realize his mother wasn't there?

He stuffed a pillow into a pillow case, straightened the bedding, then went back to the kitchen, hoping against hope that he'd imagined the whole thing.

"You need to talk to Dad," he said.

"No."

"Ma."

"No."

He gave her a steely look, but she just shook her head, then smiled wanly and patted his cheek, and headed for the bedroom. "I need sleep," she said. "I haven't slept in days."

"Me, neither," Yiannis murmured to himself.

He didn't sleep that night, either. He lay awake wondering who had turned the world upside down—and wanting Cat back in his arms.

Wanting Cat back in his life.

Just plain wanting Cat.

Cat told Adam the day after she got back to San Francisco that she couldn't marry him.

He'd come over after work, delighted that she'd realized it was time to come home, less delighted when she gave him back his ring.

"It's not you. It's me," she assured him.

And being Adam and totally confident in his own appeal, he believed her. He even smiled faintly. "I thought you were having second thoughts when you dragged your feet looking for a dress. You knew the society life wasn't for you."

Was that what had done it? Hadn't it been Yiannis at all?

It was a comforting thought. Cat hoped that Adam knew her better than she knew herself.

"You'll still come to the ball with me, won't you?"

She blinked. "You still want me to?"

"Well, you have a dress now, and I don't have a date." He spread his hands and gave her a hopeful smile.

And Cat, surprised but also surprisingly rational, decided she could do that. "I'm not changing my mind—"

"I understand."

"—and if you're sure you want me to."

"Of course. Why not?"

Indeed, why not? She had nothing else to look forward to. And it gave her something to talk to Gran about when she called her on the phone in the evening. She didn't mention breaking the engagement. There would be time for that when she saw Gran in person.

She didn't think Gran would be that surprised. Or unhappy.

She wasn't unhappy herself. Not about breaking things off with Adam.

It was Yiannis she was unhappy about, Yiannis whom she couldn't get out of her mind day or night. Three years ago when she'd left after he'd declared he had no interest in marriage, she'd done her best to move on as quickly as possible, to not let herself think about him, to resolutely put him out of her mind.

"How'd that work for you?" she asked herself sardonically now.

Well, it hadn't.

So now she faced the emotions squarely. She let herself wallow in her misery. She dragged out every memory and played it over and over in her mind. She remembered the laughter, the loving. She remembered the tears.

Maybe, if she wallowed long enough, she'd get fed up, get over it. But she suspected she wouldn't. She feared that she'd be spending her life missing Yiannis, unless God somehow granted her amnesia.

It was a good thing she had the kids at the library story hours. There was no way you could be miserable around kids. They were so relentlessly in the moment that she had to be, too. And if the two-year-old boy called Jackson in her

Wednesday morning story hour reminded her of Harry so much that she got a lump in her throat every time she looked at him, he also made her laugh.

But she was afraid, as she sat the next evening on the sofa beneath the window, sipping her tea and watching old Mrs Wang on the porch across the street combing her cat, that in another fifty years that would be her.

It wasn't a comforting thought.

His parents' marriage was not his problem.

Yiannis tried telling himself that all night. But as much as he tried to make himself believe it, he didn't.

He'd taken them for granted his whole life. They were the ones who had given him the love and support—and family—he had always depended on. Cat had envied him—and he hadn't understood why. Until now.

Now he felt he owed it to her—as well as to them—to do whatever he could to bring them together again.

But they didn't make it easy for him.

His mother denied that she was throwing away her life. "I'm getting *my* life," she said. "I've spent the last forty years living your father's."

"You don't love him?" He felt ill. And talking about love unnerved him. But somehow it was important to ask. Important to know.

"Of course I love him, the stupid old goat! But I don't love his businesses. And I don't love him being so selfish that he does what he wants without caring how it affects anyone else! I love him, but I'm going to lose him." She blinked furiously and swiped at her eyes.

"You're not going to lose him. You're divorcing him."

"Because I refuse to sit by and watch him kill himself."

"It's better to leave?" He couldn't see that.

"Yes," his mother said firmly. "It is. Staying is killing me a little bit every day."

The whole debacle was killing him, Yiannis thought grimly by the next night when his father still hadn't called and his mother had shown no signs of weakening.

But the more he listened, the more he understood her feelings. She and Cat had a lot in common. They were both loving, giving women—until pushed beyond the breaking point. Which meant that he had a lot more in common with his father than he wanted to believe. They were both selfish, blind, stubborn men.

He didn't want to call his father. They hadn't had much to say to each other in years. His father was, as his mother said, all about business. And once Socrates had determined that Yiannis was not going to be the child to pick up the reins of the family business and allow his father to run not only the business, but his life, he'd largely ignored him.

But he'd been there. Both his parents had been there for him and for his siblings so completely that he'd never ever given their support a thought. He owed them.

"I'm going to call Dad, Ma," he said.

It was just past seven o'clock Thursday night, past ten in New York provided his father was there. Time enough for him to finally get home from the office if he was coming. As the hours passed his mother had looked sadder and more depressed than ever.

Now she looked up at him, her mouth pressed in a thin tight line. Her face was bleak. She didn't say a word.

"If you don't want me to, you're going to have to tell me no now," he said, not sure if he prayed she would—or wouldn't.

She sighed, then bent her head over her clicking needles. He thought he heard her say, "I don't know what good it will do."

Yiannis didn't know, either. He stood in the doorway

watching her for a long moment. He told himself again that it wasn't his fight. But that wasn't true.

It was.

He loved his mother. He loved his irascible driven father. He loved all his siblings, his countless aunts and uncles and cousins—all his family, even the ones he wished wouldn't drop in on him without warning.

He loved them without thinking, without ever contemplating what his life would be like without them. He couldn't imagine life without them.

He would do this for all of them. And for himself.

And for Cat.

Because he was finally beginning to understand what drove her. He thought he knew now what she'd hoped he would say on Tuesday morning. And it had nothing to do with Adam. It had to do with Yiannis's own growing realization of how much she meant to him, how much he loved her.

He wanted to tell her. Needed to tell her.

But he couldn't. Not yet. Not until he'd stopped being selfish and at least made the effort to get his parents to talk to each other.

So he drew a breath, girded his loins, laid on all the emotional armor he could manage and went into his workshop where it was private, and called his father.

"Dad," he said when Socrates picked up on the first ring and his father's gruff voice barked, "Savas," in his ear. "It's Yiannis."

There was a split second's hesitation. Then, "Do you know where your mother is?"

Yiannis breathed again. "As a matter of fact I do." Another breath. "She's here."

"In California?" His father sounded somewhere been gutted and relieved. "What the hell is she doing there? You sick?"

"No. She is," Yiannis said, daring to be blunt because he knew his father. "Of you."

There was a stunned silence. Then bluster. But Yiannis knew that bluster. He'd done his own share.

"Stop being so damn selfish."

"Selfish? I work sixty hours a week. More. I do it for her. For you!"

"Yes. And for you, too," Yiannis corrected him. "It's what you bring to the family, yes? It makes you feel worthwhile."

"I am worthwhile," Socrates said flatly.

"Of course you are. But not just for business. Mom loves you," he said with quiet intensity. "Too much to watch you self-destruct. She won't do that. You shouldn't make her."

"It's all about me?" A bit of scornful bluster was back now.

"It's about the two of you and the marriage you've made. Forty years, Dad. That's a hell of a feat. I'm in awe. I never really thought about it before. Even if I had, I guess I'd have thought it just happened, that it came easy." But it hadn't. He knew that now. All the time he'd been talking to his father, he'd been talking to himself. "Don't throw it away, Dad."

"I'm not the one who left."

"Don't let her go. Don't waste your chance at happiness. Give each other another chance."

He didn't know if it did any good or not. His father made no promises. He grumbled about Lena never understanding him. He blustered about kids who didn't appreciate how hard he'd worked for them.

Yiannis let him talk. He listened. He heard the selfishness in his father's words and the pain his father was refusing to admit, doing his best to disguise.

He'd been there himself—with another woman—just days before. A woman who had left him because he'd been too damned selfish.

A woman he desperately wanted to go after and ask her to reconsider. But he'd had his chance. Not once, but twice.

Three years ago, Cat had offered him her heart, her love, her life—and he had declined.

And again, two days ago, he'd had another chance. To love her. To admit that what they'd done that night had virtually nothing to do with Adam Landry and everything to do with how Yiannis felt about Catriona MacLean.

He loved her—and because he had been so sure he wanted nothing of the sort, that he had all the family he needed, he hadn't really understood how much it meant to her.

Now he knew.

And he knew how much it meant to him. He knew how badly he wanted what his parents were in danger of throwing away. He wouldn't take it lightly. He swore to himself he wouldn't.

If he got another chance he wanted it all. Love. Marriage. Responsibility. Commitment. Children. Grandchildren.

Dear God, was he actually thinking in terms of *grandchildren*?

Yeah, he thought, rubbing a hand through his hair, he was. But he'd settle for a couple or three red-headed freckle-faced hellions of his own first. The notion made him smile at the same time it made his stomach hurt.

Because after the mess he'd made of things, it all came down to if Cat would have him.

It was a very big if.

The knock came just past noon on Saturday.

Yiannis had spent the morning trying to figure out how he could go to San Francisco and still be supportive of his mother. He'd finally figured out the answer by asking himself what Cat would do.

Take her with you.

He could hear Cat say the words, could envision the equable shrug, the "it's obvious" look on her face.

The very idea made him wince. He abhorred the thought of baring his soul to his mother, explaining why he was dragging her off to San Francisco. Besides, he knew if he did, she wouldn't do the polite thing and decline to come.

She'd want to meet Cat. She'd love to lay her eyes on the woman who had made her youngest son change his tune about marriage. He didn't want to mention the word *marriage* to his mother. But if he had to, he had to—because more than anything, he had to talk to Cat.

The knock on the door grew more imperious.

Irritated, Yiannis yanked it open.

His father strode in, his gaze darting from side to side as if he might see his wife hiding behind a chair. "Where is she?"

Yiannis shut the door and regarded his bull-headed father. "Hello to you, too."

His father jerked a curt nod in his direction, then raked his hands through his disheveled black hair. "Where's your mother?"

"She went to the bakery. She should be back any minute."

The words were barely out of his mouth when the front door opened again. "They were out of bagels so I got—oh!" Color rose in her cheeks as she stared at the man in the middle of the room.

Socrates stared back. Neither spoke.

And that was eerie in itself. Yiannis couldn't remember a time when his parents had been at a loss for words. They always talked—too much, too loud, too often. Not now.

Now they just stared mulishly at each other. He wanted to bang their heads together.

"Right," he said. He took the bag of whatever his mother had got at the bakery out of her hands and thrust it at his father. "Take this to the kitchen and make Mom a cup of tea."

His father stared at him.

"The kettle's on the stove. There's hot and cold running water. It's pretty self-explanatory."

"Yiannis," his mother began.

"Let him make you tea," he said. "Then the two of you sit down and eat whatever's in here and talk to each other. Listen to each other, too. And I hope to God you put this marriage back together. I've got to go."

He turned on his heel, strode into his bedroom, threw some clothes in a duffel bag, grabbed his jacket out of the closet and headed for the door. Neither of them had moved.

"I can't fix this for you," he told them. "You have to do that yourselves. Wish me luck."

"Luck?" his parents echoed.

"Why, Yiannis? Where are you going?"

He swallowed. "To lay my heart on the line."

The ball was like a fairy tale.

Waterfalls of glass icicles on tiered chandeliers, gold-plated fixtures, floor-to-ceiling views out over the rolling green golf course near where Adam's boss lived. Men in black tie and pristine white shirts, women in long sleek evening dresses that glittered and sparkled.

And for once in such a setting Cat didn't look out of place. The dress was perfect as she'd known it would be. In it Cat actually felt beautiful. Even Adam thought she'd made the right choice. He looked pleased to be seen with her. They made a stunning couple. Adam was by far the handsomest man in the room.

It could be a fairy tale for real—except Cat's one true love was hundreds of miles away living his life as a toad.

While the outside of Cat beamed and inside her brain she sang Bibbidi Bobbidi Boo, the truth was, life wasn't a fairy tale.

You did what you could, and that was that.

She'd done the right thing breaking off her engagement. She knew it. Adam knew it. And even though she would be going into her apartment alone, she made an effort to enjoy the evening as much as she could.

There was no reason not to. It was all perfectly lovely—the food, the orchestra, the setting. The charitable cause that the ball was in aid of was one she believed in. She'd made as big a donation as she could herself.

And she drank everything in so she could call and tell Gran about it tomorrow. She knew her grandmother would be eager to hear all about it—the music, the dresses, the men she danced with.

Even though she'd come with Adam, she danced with others. Some of them were men whose photos she saw in the newspaper financial and society pages. They went out of their way to be charming.

Adam told her she'd impressed them. "You're a success."

He looked pleased. She was, too, on his behalf. She was glad she had come if it helped him, and glad she'd had the experience. And the dances.

She'd never danced with Yiannis.

There were so many things she'd never done with him. Would never do with him.

"Getting tired?" Adam asked, apparently noting the shadow that passed over her features.

Cat pasted a smile back on her face, but nodded. "A bit."

"We can go if you want."

"Whenever you want to." It was his event. His decision. She would stay as long as he wanted. It didn't matter to her. It wasn't as if she had anything to come home to. The ball was a welcome distraction from the misery of her own company.

But Adam was ready to go.

He fetched her shawl. "You were right about that, too," he said, smoothing it lightly over her shoulders. "It does look like starlight."

Cat smiled. It was nice to be right about something—even if that something didn't matter.

In Adam's car, she closed her eyes on the way back to the city. Neither of them spoke. There was nothing to say. The night had gone well. Now it was over. This might even be the last time she would see him.

It was after one by the time they got back to the city and the car climbed the hill toward the narrow sharp-roofed, bay-windowed row house in which she lived. She'd left the light on in the front parlor of her third floor apartment. But the porch light was off. The family who lived on that level was already in bed.

"I won't come in," Adam said as he drew up in front of her house.

He didn't even shut the ignition off. He just popped the locks so they would open and said, "Good night, Cat." He leaned close and brushed a kiss across her cheek, then straightened abruptly. "Thanks for coming. Good-bye."

Good-bye?

Just like that?

She stared at him, surprised. She was glad that he understood, that he knew it was over, too. She was glad he didn't press. But she was a bit taken aback that he didn't get out and see her to her door. He had always been that kind of gentleman before.

But before the thought had barely had time to form, the car door on her side opened abruptly.

"Good night, Landry." The voice was hard, gruff and—

Yiannis?

Cat whipped around and stared up into the shadows that hid his face.

"I thought that was you when we drove up," Adam said equably. "Good night, Savas," he added as Yiannis took Cat's hand and drew her, mind reeling, out of the car and onto the sidewalk. "Good luck."

"I'm sure I'll need it," Yiannis replied grimly, shutting the door but, with his other hand, still holding Cat's arm as if he was afraid she'd run away.

She turned to face him under the street lamp. He looked hard and fierce and hollow-eyed. His lean cheeks were unshaven. He didn't look happy. In fact, he looked about as miserable as she had been.

She stared at him, wished he would say something. Her heart was pounding crazily. She felt breathless, dazed. "What are you—?"

"It's freezing out here," he broke in. "Can we go in?"

"I— Yes. Of course." He was wearing jeans and a T-shirt and a thin jacket. All right for Southern California. Not so good for San Francisco in March. She led him up the front steps, unlocked the door and brought him in. The staircase was steep and narrow. "How long have you been here?" she asked over her shoulder as she preceded him.

"Five, six hours."

She spun around and stared. "Five or six *hours*?"

He shrugged irritably. "I didn't think you'd be at the damn ball. I thought you'd finished with him."

"Because you proved to me that I didn't love him?"

She thought she heard him grind his teeth. She wasn't sure she wanted him in her apartment at all if they were just going to fight this all out again.

But before she could make her stand, he took the key out of her hand, unlocked the door himself, pushed it open and bent his head. "After you."

It was all she could do not to kick him in the shins. As it was, she went in just far enough to turn and glare at him as he shut the door behind them. "Why don't you tell me why you're here?"

He didn't. He didn't say anything. He only succeeded in making her living room feel the size of a hamster cage as he paced and prowled its confines.

Then at last he stopped and stared at her. "You look beautiful." It sounded like an accusation.

"Thank you." She stood there—looking beautiful—and didn't back down. Met his gaze, refused to look away, waited for him to say whatever he had to say.

"This isn't about Landry."

"I'm glad to hear it." At least this time they could fight about something else.

"I know you wouldn't marry him."

Still she waited.

"Will you marry me?"

Maybe the music had been too loud at the ball. She hadn't thought so. But clearly she wasn't hearing right. She stared, sure she'd misheard. "Harry's what?" she said because that must have been what he was saying.

"Damn it." The words seemed torn from him. "I said, will you marry—m.a.r.r.y—me?

Okay, that time Cat heard him. She looked around for somewhere to sit down. The closest chair was two steps away. She made it. Barely. Had he really asked her to marry him?

Yes. He had. But even knowing she hadn't mistaken the words, she wasn't sure she believed it. Or that he did.

This was the man who didn't believe in marriage, after all.

She swallowed. Looked up at him. "Why?"

Yiannis rubbed a hand over his face, took a breath, then plunged in. "Because I love you. Because I want a life with you. Because I want to wake up with you in the morning, and go to bed with you at night. Because I want to talk to you and listen to you and make love with you and have kids and grandkids with you. How's that—for a start?" He looked at her, anguished, still standing on the other side of the room.

Thank God she was sitting down. It might have been the fact that he was still on the other side of the room that made her believe him. He'd made no attempt to sway her with his undeniable physical charms. There had been no kisses, no touches.

Nothing but words.

The right words.

She laughed shakily. "Starters? There's more? You had me at 'I love you.'"

And then he was there, beside her, kneeling by the chair, wrapping his arms around her. "Oh, God, Cat, are you sure?"

She'd never been more sure of anything in her life. He'd been too honest before for her to doubt him now. "Yes," she said. "Oh, yes."

Then she dragged him up again, and he scooped her into his arms and settled in the chair with her in his lap. She tore off his jacket and fumbled the buttons of his shirt. He put his hands on her sparkly midnight sky dress and then groaned.

"I don't even know how this thing works."

"Simple," Cat said and she stood, found the hidden zipper, slid it down, did a quick shimmy and the dress simply pooled at her feet.

"I like it," Yiannis said hoarsely and then he drew her back again.

But Cat had a better idea. She took him by the hand and led him to her bedroom where he finished undressing her, then shrugged off his jeans and shorts, and fell with her onto the bed.

Their love-making was fast and furious this time. Hungry. Desperate. As if they could not get enough.

And after, lying with him on the bed, stroking her hand

down his side as he lay looking at her, Cat wondered if she would ever get enough of this man.

He ran his hand over her hair, tangled his fingers in her annoying curls and kissed them. "Beautiful," he murmured. Then he lifted his gaze and met hers. "Mine," he said, like the king of the beasts she'd seen in him.

"Yours," she agreed. "I always have been."

He nodded. "I know. I understand now. A little, at least."

"What do you mean? How?" Because whatever it was that he understood, it had brought him back to her.

He told her, then, about his mother, about his father. About suddenly realizing how much he'd complained about what he'd always taken for granted. "I was selfish," he told her frankly. "I wanted the comforts of family, the support of family. I always knew they were there—usually more of them than I wanted," he admitted wryly. "I never stopped to think about what went into making that family. Now I do."

"But he's there now? Your dad? I mean, they've worked it out?" she asked him urgently because he hadn't been lying about the pain their separation had caused him. She'd heard it in his voice, seen it in his face.

"I hope to God they have," he said. "I was tempted to call them while I was sitting on your doorstep."

"You should have!"

But he shook his head. "No. I did my bit. I told them how much they mean to all of us. I know how much they mean to each other. But they have to find the words." He paused and a corner of his mouth tipped as he played with her hair. "I had to find the words—and the guts to say them."

"I'm glad you did," Cat told him, leaning in to kiss him, to breathe the words against his lips. "I'm so very very glad you did."

His lips smiled against hers. "Me, too."

* * *

"Enough family for you?" Yiannis asked his new bride.

They were standing on the deck of his parents' house on Long Island, taking in the sea and the sand and the two hundred or so brothers, sisters, nieces, nephews, aunts, uncles, cousins and assorted Savases and in-laws whose connections he'd never entirely figured out.

"They're all yours," he told her expansively with a grin. "My wedding present to you."

Cat laughed and put her arms around him and lifted up the inch or so she needed to touch her lips to his. "I love them, each and every one," she told him, eyes dancing.

Her eyes had been dancing all week. Ever since he'd put an engagement ring on her finger. It had been his mother's ring.

"An heirloom," his mother had told him laughing through tears as she'd pressed it on him when he'd told her he was getting married. "Your father says we're making a new beginning, that he's becoming a new man, so he's giving me a new one."

"I don't want to take your first one," Yiannis had protested.

"You're not taking, I'm giving," his mother had said. "But only if your Cat wants it."

Of course Cat had wanted it. She loved his parents. And they loved her. She was going to be a daughter of the heart to his mother. And she could wrap Socrates around her little finger with nothing more than a smile.

"I think you've got this family thing figured out," he'd told her.

"I'm learning," Cat had assured him.

They'd had a small intimate wedding, just the two of them, Cat's grandmother, Yiannis's parents and Misty and Harry because Devin was back in the field somewhere.

"If we knew where, he'd have to kill us," Cat had told

Yiannis, laughing when she'd got off the phone from inviting Misty. She hugged him. "I'm so glad they're coming."

"Me, too. Maybe Harry will remember us."

"He wouldn't forget in a couple of weeks. And Misty says she tells him about us all the time. She says he loves his bunny," she added, her expression growing serious. "Thank you for sending him the rabbit."

Yiannis had smiled. "Every boy needs a rabbit," he said and kissed the tip of her nose.

And every girl—at least the one he'd married—needed a never-ending family like this one. He'd promised her his the night he'd asked her to be his wife.

But he didn't think she had really understood the scope of it until today. Now in the midst of Malena Savas's Mother's Day cum wedding reception cum family reunion, she couldn't move without tripping over some relation.

He even met one he'd never met before.

"Daniel," his brother George said, introducing them to his five-week-old son.

"Can I hold him?" Cat had asked, and Daniel was duly deposited in her arms. The maternal bit still looked good on her. She seemed almost to glow.

"You're up for the godfather bit, are you?" George asked. He sounded pleased, but a bit surprised that Yiannis had agreed.

Yiannis nodded. "I am."

"It'll be good practice for him." Cat looked up from admiring baby Daniel.

George raised a brow. "Will it now?"

And Yiannis, as the meaning of her words penetrated his thick skull, felt as if he'd been punched in the chest. "Cat?" He stared at her.

She really was glowing. And smiling. Not at George. At him.

"A baby?" He felt a shaft of panic, followed by one of elation.

"Our very own," Cat said, putting her arms around him, leaning her head against his chest. And Yiannis drew her close and kissed her hair, and tried to imagine the child they had made. He couldn't begin to.

But then, he hadn't imagined any of this.

Against his chest, Cat was humming a song he recognized. He listened closely, then he smiled.

It was indeed a beautiful day.

* * * * *

Mills & Boon® Hardback
March 2012

ROMANCE

Roccanti's Marriage Revenge	Lynne Graham
The Devil and Miss Jones	Kate Walker
Sheikh Without a Heart	Sandra Marton
Savas's Wildcat	Anne McAllister
The Argentinian's Solace	Susan Stephens
A Wicked Persuasion	Catherine George
Girl on a Diamond Pedestal	Maisey Yates
The Theotokis Inheritance	Susanne James
The Good, the Bad and the Wild	Heidi Rice
The Ex Who Hired Her	Kate Hardy
A Bride for the Island Prince	Rebecca Winters
Pregnant with the Prince's Child	Raye Morgan
The Nanny and the Boss's Twins	Barbara McMahon
Once a Cowboy...	Patricia Thayer
Mr Right at the Wrong Time	Nikki Logan
When Chocolate Is Not Enough...	Nina Harrington
Sydney Harbour Hospital: Luca's Bad Girl	Amy Andrews
Falling for the Sheikh She Shouldn't	Fiona McArthur

HISTORICAL

Untamed Rogue, Scandalous Mistress	Bronwyn Scott
Honourable Doctor, Improper Arrangement	Mary Nichols
The Earl Plays With Fire	Isabelle Goddard
His Border Bride	Blythe Gifford

MEDICAL

Dr Cinderella's Midnight Fling	Kate Hardy
Brought Together by Baby	Margaret McDonagh
The Firebrand Who Unlocked His Heart	Anne Fraser
One Month to Become a Mum	Louisa George

0212 GEN STD HB

ROMANCE

The Power of Vasilii	Penny Jordan
The Real Rio D'Aquila	Sandra Marton
A Shameful Consequence	Carol Marinelli
A Dangerous Infatuation	Chantelle Shaw
How a Cowboy Stole Her Heart	Donna Alward
Tall, Dark, Texas Ranger	Patricia Thayer
The Boy is Back in Town	Nina Harrington
Just An Ordinary Girl?	Jackie Braun

HISTORICAL

The Lady Gambles	Carole Mortimer
Lady Rosabella's Ruse	Ann Lethbridge
The Viscount's Scandalous Return	Anne Ashley
The Viking's Touch	Joanna Fulford

MEDICAL

Cort Mason – Dr Delectable	Carol Marinelli
Survival Guide to Dating Your Boss	Fiona McArthur
Return of the Maverick	Sue MacKay
It Started with a Pregnancy	Scarlet Wilson
Italian Doctor, No Strings Attached	Kate Hardy
Miracle Times Two	Josie Metcalfe

Mills & Boon® Hardback

April 2012

ROMANCE

A Deal at the Altar	Lynne Graham
Return of the Moralis Wife	Jacqueline Baird
Gianni's Pride	Kim Lawrence
Undone by his Touch	Annie West
The Legend of de Marco	Abby Green
Stepping out of the Shadows	Robyn Donald
Deserving of his Diamonds?	Melanie Milburne
Girl Behind the Scandalous Reputation	Michelle Conder
Redemption of a Hollywood Starlet	Kimberly Lang
Cracking the Dating Code	Kelly Hunter
The Cattle King's Bride	Margaret Way
Inherited: Expectant Cinderella	Myrna Mackenzie
The Man Who Saw Her Beauty	Michelle Douglas
The Last Real Cowboy	Donna Alward
New York's Finest Rebel	Trish Wylie
The Fiancée Fiasco	Jackie Braun
Sydney Harbour Hospital: Tom's Redemption	Fiona Lowe
Summer With A French Surgeon	Margaret Barker

HISTORICAL

Dangerous Lord, Innocent Governess	Christine Merrill
Captured for the Captain's Pleasure	Ann Lethbridge
Brushed by Scandal	Gail Whitiker
Lord Libertine	Gail Ranstrom

MEDICAL

Georgie's Big Greek Wedding?	Emily Forbes
The Nurse's Not-So-Secret Scandal	Wendy S. Marcus
Dr Right All Along	Joanna Neil
Doctor on Her Doorstep	Annie Claydon

0312 GEN STD HB

ROMANCE

Jewel in His Crown	Lynne Graham
The Man Every Woman Wants	Miranda Lee
Once a Ferrara Wife...	Sarah Morgan
Not Fit for a King?	Jane Porter
Snowbound with Her Hero	Rebecca Winters
Flirting with Italian	Liz Fielding
Firefighter Under the Mistletoe	Melissa McClone
The Tycoon Who Healed Her Heart	Melissa James

HISTORICAL

The Lady Forfeits	Carole Mortimer
Valiant Soldier, Beautiful Enemy	Diane Gaston
Winning the War Hero's Heart	Mary Nichols
Hostage Bride	Anne Herries

MEDICAL

Breaking Her No-Dates Rule	Emily Forbes
Waking Up With Dr Off-Limits	Amy Andrews
Tempted by Dr Daisy	Caroline Anderson
The Fiancée He Can't Forget	Caroline Anderson
A Cotswold Christmas Bride	Joanna Neil
All She Wants For Christmas	Annie Claydon